SILENT NIGHTS AND VAMPIRE LIGHTS

A GRIMM MAWR HOLIDAY NOVELLA

SABRINA SILVERS

ABOUT SILENT NIGHTS AND VAMPIRE LIGHTS

What's cozier than a road trip with a brooding vampire who's allergic to the sun? A road trip with a brooding vampire at Christmastime, obviously.

Holly Winters is on the run, and not just from the loneliness of the season—this time, it's from the mob. Witnessing a hit has landed her on the naughty list of some very dangerous men. Her Christmas escape plan goes off the rails when she's cornered at a snowy train station. Enter Nicholas Frost: tall, dark, mysterious, and just a little undead. He saves her life, but his price for protection? Holly has to drive him home.

For Nicholas, this road trip is nothing but a means to an end. He's a centuries-old vampire with no interest in sugar cookies, snowmen, or the ceaseless hum of Christmas carols coming from the human woman in the driver's seat. But as they navigate festive small-town stops and late-night conversations, Holly's holiday cheer begins to thaw his frosty demeanor.

Holly isn't sure what's crazier: that she's road-tripping with a vampire, or that her grumpy, gorgeous passenger is somehow inspiring all kinds of holiday feelings she wasn't expecting. And Nicholas? He's starting to wonder if maybe, just maybe, this sassy, sunshine-filled human is the greatest gift he never knew he needed.

Get ready for a road trip full of Yuletide cheer, irresistible banter, and some very heated silent nights!

Copyright © December 2024 by Sabrina Silvers

Cover by Erin Dameron-Hill

All rights reserved.

This book is a work of fiction. Names, characters, places, and incidents either are a product of the author's imagination or used fictitiously. Any resemblance to actual people, living or dead, or businesses, events or locales is entirely coincidental. Any mistakes are the author's own and may be intentional and fictional.

No part of this book may be reproduced in any form or by any electronic or mechanical means, including information storage and retrieval systems, without written permission from the author, except for the use of brief quotations in a book review.

CHAPTER 1

NICHOLAS

A train whistle pierced the early morning air in the small Pennsylvania train station. The sun had not yet risen, so I was safe, for now, but I wouldn't be for much longer if I didn't get on the damned train. It had been late pulling into the station, and I risked the sun coming up, but I still had time. Something, however, poked at my brain, telling me something was wrong. Not with me, but just a vague sense of unease that wouldn't let me get on the train.

Of course, the reason I was getting on the train could cause this sense of nervousness. I crinkled the piece of paper in my hand and resisted the urge to throw it in the garbage can a few feet away. Throwing it away wouldn't erase the message, no matter how much I wanted to ignore it. The universe had already allowed me to ignore it for several weeks since it had been mailed via the slowest route possible —the postal service and all the different address changes I'd left behind over the many years since I'd left home. An email or text message would have been far easier and more direct, though those methods were too modern for my family, mired as they were in the past. Granted, I may have forgotten to give them my updated cell phone number, though I used it so rarely that I often forgot it myself.

Or had I? Honestly, I didn't remember. It had been decades since I'd been home, but I kept in touch with our family's blood servants, so they knew I was still alive. They always knew how to contact me. Or at least I thought so. Vampires, along with other supernatural creatures, had only come out in the past few decades. Prior to then, I had had to keep moving, changing my identity frequently to reduce questions about my lack of aging. Now, things were infinitely easier. I resumed my original name and traveled as I wanted, though only at night. That curse still affected me, as it did all vampires.

Which was why I was seated on this cold, plastic bench in the middle of a rural Pennsylvania waiting for the train to begin my long journey home. Though it wasn't the only reason.

I was tired. I had been alone for a long time, making my way through the states, helping people, trying to smooth relations between the vampire community and humans. Initially, I had done it under a cloak of secrecy, since vampires were only a myth, an urban legend. When we revealed ourselves, things didn't get much better. Some humans welcomed us, while others hunted us. And our kind reacted just as badly. For too long, the vampire community had seen humans as foes or food. We needed to find common ground to build relations.

I had been so naïve, telling that to my father and the head of our clan, my cousin Hugo. They both told me I was young, arrogant, inexperienced. Those were the kind words. Other words were stupid, ignorant, simple. But I was determined to prove them wrong. Had I succeeded? Doubtful. All I knew was that I was tired, and I needed a place where I could be safe, where I could retreat for a while and know that I didn't have to be on guard all the time. I had to go home. Based on this letter, I was welcome.

Slowly, I smoothed the crinkled paper, folded it carefully into four sections, and tucked it into the inside pocket of my leather jacket. I stood, slung my duffel bag over my shoulder, and made my way to the train to find the sleeper car I'd booked for the trip. This railway made special accommodations for vampires. Between that and an extra donation, I would be protected while in my deep sleep during the day, then have a delightful dinner of warmed blood waiting for me. Bagged, not fresh. No one wanted a hungry vampire on a train.

I paused as I took a step up, that feeling of unease prodding at my senses. Then I caught a delicate, fresh scent on the breeze. The smell of sugar cookies, cinnamon, and vanilla teased my senses, and my fangs pressed against my gums, igniting a hunger even though I'd already fed well that evening. I glanced behind me, scanning the surrounding platform area and parking lot, but didn't catch sight of the source of the delectable fragrance.

"Can you keep it moving, buddy?" A man behind me gave me a little push, and I froze and slowly pivoted, staring him down. The man paled and stumbled back, dropping his carry-on and holding his hands up. "S-sorry, man. Take your time."

I silenced the rumble in my chest, not realizing I had even let it start, and got on the train. But the whisper of unease wouldn't leave me. As I made my way down the aisle of the regular car, towards the sleeper in the back, I peered out the windows into the darkness, cursing the blinding lights around the platform that hindered my night vision.

Then I saw it. A figure in white, moving quickly, running even. But two darker figures reached her first and hauled her back into the shadows. No one was around. No one saw. I was the only witness.

I whirled around and pushed past the man behind me, shoving him into a woman already seated, barely offering a muttered apology. Something told me that I had to save her, or I would regret it forever. I'd spent much of my long years in a similar capacity, dispensing justice and helping others as I saw fit. But nothing was more imperative than this moment.

The train doors began to close, and the car jerked. The engine's sound changed in preparation to pull out. "Buddy, you can't get off now. You'll be killed!"

The ticket inspector stood in my way, blocking the exit, but I hissed, my fangs fully engaged and eyes red from the blood lust surging inside. The man stumbled back, terrified by the sight.

The doors to the platform were closing, and I wrenched them open, shoving my way through, my bag catching for a second on the doors. I jumped from the moving train, landing on the platform on my hands and knees, barely feeling the impact. I scrambled to my feet, my gaze already fixed on where the woman had been dragged. I inhaled, opening my senses. The smell of gun oil, garlic, and fear overpowered the sweeter scents I had first detected.

Leaving my bag where it had landed next to me, I sprinted for the darkness, a blinding speed that only a vampire could make, a growl emanating from me. *Mine*.

Holly

I trembled as I scanned the train station parking lot in the early December morning. I was bone-weary, every muscle in my body aching with exhaustion. As a baker, I was used to early mornings, but that was usually after an early night to bed. Not after being chased for days by mobsters determined to silence me for what I'd seen almost a week ago in the alley behind the bakery where I worked.

The police had tried to help me, but they needed time to verify my story. Wasn't it enough that Mr. Dimitriou hadn't opened his shop all week and hadn't been home? Did they really believe he suddenly took a trip for his health? His health was terrible because I saw him shot dead in the alley! No more would I ration his pastries because of his diabetes or worry about his high blood pressure. He didn't have to worry about that anymore. But I felt terrible for his poor wife, who didn't know what had happened to him. Though when I saw her two days ago and looked into her eyes, she knew but was too terrified to speak of it.

And now someone was making sure I could never speak of it, either. I had to leave the bakery, the one place where I had thought I might be able to put down some roots. Now I had to figure out where to go next. Where would I be safe? I had no family, few friends, and nowhere to go. Theoretically, that should make it harder for the guys on my tail to track me, right? They couldn't predict my actions. Yet somehow, they'd been everywhere I had gone in the past few days—the bus station, police station, my apartment, a hotel in town. I had hoped they would either be sleeping or working at this time, and I could slip out of town.

So far, so good.

I grabbed the one bag I had been able to salvage from my apartment. I didn't dare go back for anything else, not after I had walked in on them ransacking my place. I had fled with only the bag and my car. Now to get the hell out of Dodge, as the saying went.

I only saw a few solitary figures, men and women in business attire, probably taking the train to the city or on a business trip. No one else lingering anywhere. No cars off to the side. I had been sitting and waiting for two hours until the train pulled up. When the whistle went off, my heart almost exploded in my chest. But now I could escape. Make a new life somewhere else and hope they couldn't find me.

After debating for a few more minutes, I grabbed my bag, got out of my car, and raced for the train, only to be yanked back just at the edge of the parking lot. I screamed, but a leather glove slapped over my mouth, cutting off the sound.

"Be quiet or we'll have to make you be quiet," a menacing voice spoke from the darkness behind me.

"I thought we were doing that, anyway. Aren't we going to kill her, Tommy?" the other voice, more high-pitched but still male, asked.

There was a slapping sound, and the high-pitched male yelled, "Ow, what was that for?"

"For you being a dumbass. Shut your mouth and grab her bag. We gotta go before anyone sees us," Tommy, I presumed, said, terrifying me.

I wiggled hard, wrenching around like the trout I once saw flopping on the boat when my grandpa took me fishing. My thrashing must have surprised them because suddenly the hold eased, and I darted away, yelling for someone to help me.

Only there was no one left. The station was deserted, and the train was pulling away. The high-pitch, piercing warble of the whistle drowned out my screams as the train, and my hope, chugged away.

I was going to die here. All alone. No one would care. I

had no one left. My parents had died when I was young, and my grandparents had taken me in, raising me until their deaths. I had no one else. I would be forgotten. And at the happiest time of the year.

Christmas.

Didn't that just suck?

CHAPTER 2

NICHOLAS

Once I passed the platform lights, my vision adjusted to the darkness, and there she was—running straight for me. No, not for me specifically. She was running for safety, any safety. Not everyone considered vampires safe, and we weren't. Not unless we wanted to be.

And tonight, I didn't want to be.

I'd fed earlier, so hunger wasn't my issue. Rage, though? That was burning through me, white-hot and all-consuming. When she was suddenly yanked back by something—her scarf, maybe, or her hair—I heard the strangled sound she made. Choking. It fueled my anger, my fangs fully descending, my growls echoing through the night. The two men didn't notice me at first, but when they did, it was too late.

The skinny one screamed—a shrill, pathetic sound—just as I slammed into him. I grabbed him by the shoulders, shook him hard enough to hear the sickening crack of bone, and flung him into the shrubs near the parking lot. He disappeared into the darkness with a distant thud.

I turned to the other one, the one holding a gun. His hand

shook as he aimed it at me, his pulse thundering loud enough to make me smile. "We don't want no trouble," he stammered. "Go on your way and nobody will get hurt."

Nobody? My gaze narrowed, the scent of blood hitting me hard. Hers. The sweet, infuriating smell of her blood—spiced with vanilla, cinnamon, and something uniquely her—combined with the sight of the split lip they'd given her.

"No one?" I repeated, my voice soft, dangerous. "So, she's free to go?"

The idiot froze, his eyes darting to her before flicking back to me. In one swift motion, I knocked the gun from his hand and sent him flying with a casual backhand. He crashed into a car, setting off its alarm. The wailing siren scraped against my nerves, an irritating reminder of how fragile and loud human things were.

I took a step toward him, ready to finish what he started, when a sound from her—just a soft, pained moan—dragged my attention away.

I turned, and there she was, trying to push herself off the ground. Her scent hit me again, stronger now, wrapping around me like a goddamn chain. Vanilla, cinnamon, and—cookies? What the hell was wrong with me?

Kneeling beside her, I studied her face, pale and terrified. "Are you okay?" I asked, my voice coming out rougher than I intended.

She gasped for air, clawing at her throat, where that ridiculous scarf was knotted tight. Knitted Santas and dancing reindeer mocked me as I realized what had happened—the bastard had yanked the scarf, choking her.

I ripped through the fabric easily, tossing it aside. She collapsed back, sucking in deep breaths and rubbing her neck, her skin marked red where the scarf had tightened.

The man? He was running now, stumbling across the

parking lot. I could've caught him in a heartbeat, but I didn't move. She had my full attention.

Then she punched me and screamed again, shaking her hand.

"You ruined my scarf!" she yelled, her voice raspy but brimming with outrage. "That was my favorite scarf!"

I gaped at her, utterly bemused. "A scarf?" I echoed. "You're angry about a scarf? Those men almost killed you."

"That scarf was important to me," she snapped, grabbing the ruined ends like she could somehow put them back together.

I barked a laugh, sharp and humorless. "Then maybe I'll leave you to their tender mercies. The other one's still around here somewhere, probably eager to finish what he started."

Her wide eyes snapped to mine, the anger draining from her face as she took in my red eyes and elongated fangs. She swayed, then fainted, collapsing right into my arms.

Oh, for fuck's sake. A fainter. Of course.

Holly

I woke up slowly, my head pounding, and realized I was lying across the backseat of a moving car. My body jolted upright, adrenaline shooting through me. What the hell? Had they grabbed me while I was out? Were they driving me to some dump site?

Wait. This looked like my car. Wadded up blanket. Bags for the grocery store. Stuffed overnight bag with my clothes haphazardly sticking out of it, including a pink bra. My favorite. What the heck?

I blinked, trying to focus on the figure behind the wheel. Big guy, easily over six feet tall, broad enough to make my Subaru Impreza look like a clown car. He was hunched over the steering wheel, hands gripping it so hard his knuckles were white. And the car? Crawling along at a snail's pace—hell, I could probably out-walk it.

He wasn't one of the creeps who'd grabbed me earlier. That much I was sure of. But was he some kind of savior, or just the next bad decision in a long line of them?

"Excuse me?" My voice was sharp, cutting through the quiet. "What do you think you're doing?"

He flinched like I'd just slapped him, his head whipping around. For a moment, he looked startled, then relief washed over his face. "Good, you're awake."

I struggled into a full sitting position, arms crossed like I could somehow shield myself from whatever fresh hell this was. "Obviously. Where are you taking me?"

"I don't know," he said, his voice low, almost sheepish. "I just need to get somewhere safe for the night."

"Join the club," I muttered, my fingers curling into fists. Then it hit me—the flash of fangs, the red eyes from earlier. I scrambled back as far as I could, pressing myself into the seat. "You're a vampire. Oh my God, you're saving me for a snack later, aren't you? Well, I'm telling you right now, I am not premium blood. I eat like crap, I don't exercise, and I'm chubby. There are way better options out there."

To my surprise, he grinned. Not a full, terrifying fang-baring grin, but just enough to make him look—well, almost handsome. "Don't worry," he said, a hint of humor in his tone. "I already ate. For today. But the sun's coming up, and I missed my train. I need somewhere safe to hole up."

"So you decided to drag me along for the ride?" My voice

pitched higher with incredulity. "What am I—dinner, a midnight snack, or something?"

"Or something."

Before I could demand clarification, a blaring horn snapped my attention to the street outside. We were stopped in the middle of the road, blocking traffic. Cars were lined up behind us, their drivers leaning on their horns. "You need to drive," I hissed. "Now."

"I don't know where to go," he admitted, his voice calm, like this wasn't a disaster waiting to happen.

I sighed, rubbing my temples. What was it about me that screamed caretaker to every stray or lost soul within a five-mile radius? First, the cats that had overrun my apartment complex and gotten me evicted, and now this guy. Fine. Whatever. "Pull into that parking lot," I said, pointing at an all-night diner. "For now."

He obeyed, turning into the lot. When he cut the engine, he twisted around to face me. "Nicholas Frost," he said. "You're in trouble."

"No shit, Sherlock." I glared at him, my frustration bubbling over. "I'm Holly Winters."

He flashed a hint of fang again, and this time his grin was less charming, more predatory. It helped that the fangs looked smaller, less scary. "I can help you."

"The police said the same thing," I shot back, bitterness seeping into my voice. "After they 'verified my story.'"

He snorted. "I'm guessing that didn't go well."

"Not exactly." I hesitated, unsure how much to tell him, but he already knew I was in trouble. "I saw something I shouldn't have, and now they're after me. I don't even know who 'they' are, but they want me dead."

My throat tightened, tears pricking at my eyes. God, I hated crying. It didn't matter if it was a Hallmark commercial, a soldier surprising his kid, or a damn animal video—I always cried. And now, in front of a vampire, of all people? Perfect. Just perfect.

To his credit, Nicholas didn't look horrified by my tears. If anything, he looked regretful. "They won't stop," he said finally. "If you stay, they'll find you. Public transportation? They'll track you down. But if you come with me, you might have a chance to escape."

I narrowed my eyes. "Go with you where?"

His expression soured, like he'd just bitten into a lemon. "Home. I've been summoned for the holidays."

"Summoned? What are you, a servant or something? Why wouldn't you want to go home? If I had a family, I'd never leave."

"Trust me, it's complicated." He sighed. "But I need to get home, and my train's gone. I need a ride. And a companion."

I frantically searched my scattered mind for what I knew about vampires. I came from a small town in western Pennsylvania. We don't have too many supernaturals and no vampires. The closest we had were a small wolf pack and a couple of orcs who all kept to themselves. As long as the wolves didn't hunt the livestock, most people were fine with them, and the orcs were great blacksmiths. But I didn't have any experience with vampires, so anything I knew came from rumors and stories. I sensed that put me at a huge disadvantage. I wished I had my phone to do some research, but I didn't see it anywhere around me.

There was one thing I had to make very clear. "I'm not a blood bank or meals on wheels," I warned.

He rolled his eyes, exasperated. "I told you—I don't want your blood. I want your driving skills. If you drive me home, I'll make sure you're safe. Completely off their radar."

"Disappear?" I raised an eyebrow. "That sounds ominous."

"It means a new identity," he said patiently. "You'll be alive, but no one will find you."

It sounded too good to be true. But what choice did I have? "Fine," I said finally. "But no nibbling on me. I mean it."

"Deal." His grin returned, this time more amused than menacing. "Shall we?"

God help me. What had I just agreed to?

CHAPTER 3

NICHOLAS

*A*s if I'd use her as a blood bag—her words, not mine —or meals on wheels. That would be reckless, not to mention insulting. It wasn't that I couldn't control myself; I could. Contrary to popular belief, most vampires don't drain their victims for sport or sustenance unless they're starving. Only the truly twisted indulge in that sort of barbarity.

I'd spent decades fighting to clean up that mess— breaking up those grotesque "parties" and ensuring humans were safe from my kind. And what did I get for it? Gratitude? No. Just stakes aimed at my heart and a never-ending supply of pitchforks. Humans were predictable like that, lumping all vampires into one bloody stereotype.

Father had warned me about this long ago. "Humans will never trust us, Nicholas. They've hunted us, witches, shifters and other monsters for centuries. They aren't open-minded creatures." And after nearly a hundred years of trying to prove him wrong, here I was, summarily exhausted and, admittedly, a little disillusioned.

The letter from my mother had been both a relief and a

burden. I wasn't eager to face Father, admit he'd been right, or endure the suffocating politics of the clan or Grimm Mawr. But I needed peace, even if I had to swallow my pride to find it.

Then there was Holly Winters, who complicated everything. Sweet, naïve Holly, who stubbornly refused to be my blood companion or servant. Without that bond, my protection over her would only go so far when we reached my family's domain. She'd be fair game. The idea of her in Grimm Mawr, surrounded by predators who wouldn't hesitate to claim her… no. I'd have to send her away before we arrived. But first, I'd keep my promise and make sure she was safe with a new identity.

When we finally reached the motel, the first rays of sunlight were already threatening the horizon. Too close. December's short days and weak sun offered some grace, but not enough. Holly stayed obediently in the room, as I'd commanded, while I succumbed to the pull of daylight.

Even in my sleep, I was aware of her. The soft hum of her voice as she sang along to holiday music on the television. The scent of her—warm and human—permeating the space. She didn't leave the room, proving she wasn't as reckless as most humans I'd encountered. Small blessings.

When the sun finally set, I woke to find her hovering over me, her blue eyes wide and curious. Before I could speak, she screamed and bolted to the other bed.

"What were you looking at?" I demanded, sitting up slowly.

Her cheeks flushed, and she stammered, "I-I was just wondering when you'd wake up. The sun went down hours ago, and you hadn't moved."

I arched a brow. "The sun hasn't fully set. My body knows exactly when it rises and falls. I wake and sleep accordingly."

She tilted her head like an inquisitive bird. "So you can't control it? Like… narcolepsy?"

I fought the urge to roll my eyes. "It's not an illness. It's biology. And I don't have to sleep."

She cocked her head. "You can stay awake?"

"We require sleep much like you do. But when the sun rises and sets, it forces our body into a form of hibernation to protect us from the harmful effects of the sun, though we do not need to sleep during our hibernation. Many of our kind choose to sleep. It's a process, similar to your… monthly cycle, only daily."

Her nose wrinkled in disgust. "Okay, let's not talk about that. You're my boss. That's weird."

"I'm not your boss," I corrected. "You're my companion."

"Nor your blood bank," she shot back. "You hired me to drive, and my payment is a new identity. Boss. Employee."

"Whatever helps you sleep at night," I muttered, standing and stretching.

She perked up, grabbing a notepad and a map. "Speaking of driving, I planned our route for tonight! Did you know there's a cute little town on the way with the best Christmas market? I thought we could stop there for the day and check it out."

I stared at her, dumbfounded. "I'm not on a Christmas tour. I need to get home before Yule." Hell, I didn't even like Christmas.

"It's on the way," she insisted. "No detours. I even reserved a room." She beamed at me as if this plan was the pinnacle of genius.

I snatched the paper from her hands, scanning the route. My jaw tightened, but I couldn't deny the logic. "It'll do. A better route than I had."

Her grin widened. "Great! I thought avoiding major cities

would make it harder for anyone to follow us. Less populated areas are easier to keep an eye on, right?"

I sighed. "Easier to see them, yes. Also easier for them to ambush us without witnesses."

Her smile faltered, and guilt pricked at me, though I didn't understand why. "But," I added, "I prefer it to overcrowded cities. It's a good plan."

Her face lit up again, and the warmth of her joy hit me square in the chest. Damn it.

"Let's go," she chirped. "We've got a lot of road ahead of us."

Holly

I hummed along with the cheery tune of "Jingle Bells" playing in the gas station as I wandered the aisles in search of road trip snacks. So many choices, so little time. When I'd asked Nicholas what he wanted, he'd just stared at me with that flat, unnerving look of his. The kind that made me think he might be sizing up my carotid artery. Not that I was about to stick around and find out. I'd slapped my hands over my neck and hurried inside before he could say anything. Did vampires even eat?

Near the counter, a display of scarves caught my eye—black and gold, with Pittsburgh logos plastered across them. Hockey? Football? I didn't know, and I didn't care. I fingered the fabric, trying to ignore the pang of loss that stabbed at me.

I missed my Santa-and-reindeer scarf. I still had the pieces, but fixing it felt impossible. Grandma had knit that scarf for me, my last tangible connection to her, and now it was ruined. Better shredded wool than my throat, sure, but it still stung.

Lately, though, keeping my neck covered felt less like a comfort and more like a necessity. Nicholas had this way of looking at me, intense and focused, and I couldn't help but wonder: if he bit me, would it hurt? Or would it be like those steamy vampire romance novels where it was… well, pleasurable?

I snatched one of the scarves off the display. Nope. Not going there. This was a job, and mixing business with pleasure was the quickest way to get myself killed—or worse. Decision made, I marched to the counter, paid for my scarf and snacks, and headed outside.

My arms were full of junk food and the ridiculous scarf as I crossed the brightly lit space between the pumps. That was when I felt it. Something hard pressed into my side, and I froze. A hand grabbed my arm, firm and unyielding.

"We're going to take this nice and slow, sweetheart. Got it?" a dark voice rasped in my ear, low and menacing. "No screaming, no calling for help. You don't want anyone else to die because of you, do you?"

I shook my head, numb. My hands clutched tighter around the snacks and the scarf as my eyes darted around. A young woman pumped gas a few feet away, a car seat visible in her back seat. A baby. Another man was at his truck, the back covered in bumper stickers for three kids, a dog, and a wife. They had people who needed them.

Then I looked for Nicholas. He was at the next pump over, putting the nozzle away. Could vampires survive gunshots? I didn't want to find out. He had a complicated relationship with his family, sure, but at least he had one. People who'd miss him.

Me? I had no one. No one would even notice if I disappeared. The only thing I could do now was keep the peace and save the others.

I swallowed hard and whispered, "Okay."

"Wise decision." The man's grip on me tightened as he began moving me toward the side of the building, away from the lights and cameras. The shadows swallowed us, and my shoulders slumped as I resigned myself to whatever was about to happen.

Then his grip slackened, just enough that I dared to turn my head.

Nicholas wasn't by the pumps anymore. Where was he? Had he gone back to the car?

Before I could say a word, a blur of movement caught my eye. Suddenly, my attacker was slammed against the wall, Nicholas's hand pinning him effortlessly. His face was inches from the man's, his fangs gleaming in the dim light.

"So kind of you to bring me dinner, Holly," Nicholas said, his voice smooth and cold. "I was starving."

Before I could even process what was happening, Nicholas sank his teeth into the man's neck. The man jerked and flailed, but he couldn't make a sound. Nicholas was too strong, too fast. When he finally pulled back, the man's body slumped, and with one sharp twist, Nicholas snapped his neck. The sickening crack echoed in the quiet night.

Nicholas tossed the body into a nearby dumpster like it was trash and turned back to me, brushing nonexistent dust from his shirt. His expression was unreadable, except for a flicker of something… predatory.

"Did you get everything you needed?" he asked, his tone calm, almost casual, as if we hadn't just crossed into full horror movie territory.

My hands shook as I clutched the stupid scarf. "Y-yeah. Everything."

CHAPTER 4

NICHOLAS

The girl didn't faint this time, which was a step up. But Holly's silence stretched so long I started to wonder if she'd cracked under the pressure. She just sat there, wide-eyed and trembling, like a fragile little bird too stunned to fly. Eventually, I reached over, gently pried the scarf and snacks from her stiff arms and walked her back to the car.

Once inside, I drove us a short distance away, parked in a quiet spot, and turned the heat on full blast. Holly was shaking so violently it made my chest tighten—not that I'd admit that to her. I draped the scarf around her neck, more for comfort than warmth, and leaned back to watch her slowly pull herself together.

The shudders eased until she was just sitting there, staring straight ahead. "You killed him," she finally said, her voice small but sharp.

I didn't flinch. "He would have killed you. Which would you have preferred?"

She turned to me, those wide eyes swimming with something between disbelief and accusation. "That none of this had happened!"

I let out a low sigh, resting my arm across the back of the seat. "I understand. But leaving him alive wasn't an option. He'd have come after you again. You know that."

Her lips parted, but no words came. She swallowed, her gaze dropping to her hands in her lap. "Others will follow."

"Maybe," I admitted with a shrug. "But I'm betting he didn't tell anyone where he found you. He wouldn't have wanted his bosses to know he failed. For now, we have a head start."

"You say that so easily," she murmured, barely audible over the hum of the heater. "How can you… do that? Kill someone like it's nothing?"

I leaned forward, resting my elbows on my knees. She had no idea. "It's not nothing. But I've been an enforcer, a soldier, for a long time. I keep our kind in line, make sure we don't overstep with humans—or each other. I don't like killing, but I'll do it when there's no other choice. And tonight, there wasn't."

Her silence dragged on, tension crackling in the confined space. Then, quietly, she said, "Thank you. For saving me. Again."

The corners of my mouth twitched, though I kept my tone flat. "You're welcome."

She hesitated, then blurted out, "When you drank from him—"

"It could have been pleasurable for him or not," I said, cutting her off. "Doesn't matter now. I saw enough in his mind to know he wouldn't have stopped hunting you. That's why I didn't wipe his memory—it's never a guarantee."

What I didn't tell her was just how twisted his plans had been. The man was scum, and his death had been a mercy—for both of us.

Holly exhaled, slow and shaky, then straightened in her seat. "Well," she said, forcing a brittle smile. "We should get back on the road. We've wasted enough time already. And the driver chooses the road trip music!"

Gods help me. I hadn't known she was a walking Christmas jukebox when I'd signed up for this. If I had, I might've reconsidered—or ripped the car's stereo out before we hit the road. But after what had just happened, I bit back my groan and let her have this one.

For an hour, maybe two, I managed. Then the third hour of festive chaos started to chip away at my sanity. Holly sang along to every song—off-key, I might add—and tried to rope me into her merry madness. I rubbed my temples as the grating lisp of "All I Want for Christmas Is My Two Front Teeth" clawed at my brain. My gums ached in solidarity. Then came "I Saw Mommy Kissing Santa Claus." The nasally whine was so unbearable I considered hurling myself out of the moving vehicle.

"You would think I was torturing you," Holly quipped, glancing at me with a wicked grin. "What are you, some kind of grinch?"

"Something like that," I muttered. "These songs are an assault on the senses. Like an icepick to the skull."

She snorted, rolling her eyes as she maneuvered the car with frustrating ease. "Oh, come on. Imagine you're a kid, sneaking downstairs to find your mom kissing Santa. That's magical!"

"What's magical about your mother cheating on your father?" I shot back.

She threw her hands up in exasperation. "It's Santa! He's on the list."

I raised an eyebrow. "The list?"

"You know, the permissions list every couple has for who they'd, uh…" Her voice trailed off, and she muttered, "Not that I'd know. It's been so long since I've had a relationship or sex, but whatever."

That last part wasn't meant for me, but my body reacted anyway. Her scent, her warmth, the pulse fluttering so enticingly beneath her skin—it was all too much. I'd fed recently, but the thought of tasting her, of feeling her blood course through me... It was dangerous. Maddening.

"A permissions list," I said, seizing on the safer topic. "Never considered one of those. Intriguing."

She shot me a suspicious look. "Do you have a Mrs. Impaler or something?"

"My name is Frost," I corrected, "and no, I do not."

"Then why would you need a list?"

I smirked, but before I could answer, she turned off the highway and onto a narrow back road. The sudden shift jarred me. "Why are we not on the highway?"

She avoided my gaze. "Thought someone was following us. Took a detour."

I gestured to the bumper-to-bumper traffic ahead. "Brilliant plan."

She ignored me, humming along to the soft strains of "It's Beginning to Look a Lot Like Christmas". For a moment, I let myself relax—until we crested a hill, and the valley below blinded me.

Lights. So many lights. Every building, every tree, every square inch of the town was drowning in a sea of blinking, glowing chaos.

"What the holy hell is this?"

Holly

*O*kay, so I hadn't exactly mentioned the slight detour to the Christmas Village. But come on—it was a huge attraction in Pennsylvania, and I'd been dying to go for years. I'd even planned to visit this season, but life, as always, got in the way. When I mapped out our route while watching Nicholas sleep—or die? Do vampires technically die during the day?—I realized we'd be passing awfully close to the village. It felt like a sign, a little Christmas miracle just for me.

I didn't believe Nicholas was as much of a Grinch as he claimed to be. Though, as we got closer, and he grouched about my choice of music, his mood made me wonder. It only made me sing louder, belting out "Jingle Bell Rock" like I was auditioning for Broadway. His red-eyed glare was enough to give me pause. Okay, maybe I'd pushed him a bit too far.

"It's on the way," I blurted, trying to sound casual. "We're only a few miles off the highway. Besides, there's an accident on the main route. We'd be stuck in traffic anyway, sitting ducks for the hitmen. This way is safer. Right? I mean, more witnesses and all…"

Nicholas closed his eyes, pinching the bridge of his nose. "Holly, for my sanity, please stop talking."

I frowned, my fingers tightening on the steering wheel. "I just wanted to see the display. It's supposed to be amazing."

He sighed like I'd asked him to walk barefoot through the snow. "We have somewhere to be, and we're entirely too close to the men tracking you. Did you think of that?"

"They wouldn't attack in front of children, would they?" My voice wavered as doubt crept in. God, what if I'd just dragged a literal vampire and a bunch of innocent kids into danger?

I glanced at the dazzling lights up ahead, all warm and

glittery, like pure holiday joy in the middle of the night. My chest tightened. "No, you're right. We should keep going."

With a sigh, I hit the blinker and started to turn the car around.

"Stop." Nicholas's hand landed on mine. "If you really want to see this monstrosity, we can spare an hour. Just an hour."

Joy exploded inside me like fireworks. "You won't regret it. It's fabulous. You might even find gifts for your family."

He grimaced. "Doubtful."

I ignored him and followed the line of cars winding toward the parking lot. Minutes later, we were walking through a wonderland of twinkling lights, holiday cheer, and more decorations than I'd ever seen. It was magical. Every worry about who might be chasing me vanished as I soaked in the laughter of kids, the scent of cinnamon and pine, and the festive music spilling from hidden speakers.

Nicholas wandered off while I watched kids giggling with Santa. When he returned, he handed me a cup. "Hot chocolate," he said, his voice gruff. "They added a peppermint stick to it for flavor."

I laughed as he glanced at his own cup, peppermint-free. "It's delicious. Like a cup of Christmas. You didn't want to try it?"

"Chocolate is a flavor. Why add something else?" He frowned, clearly baffled by the concept.

His confusion made me laugh harder. "Try it," I said, holding my cup up to his lips. "You might like it, even if you don't like Christmas."

"I never said I don't like Christmas," he muttered before reluctantly taking a sip.

I raised an eyebrow. "You hate the music, didn't want to come here, clearly don't want to go home, and you're wearing literally nothing festive. You're a total Grinch. Now, admit it—peppermint makes it better."

He swallowed, his face begrudging. "It's... unique."

"Ha! I'll take it. But you can't have mine. You're stuck with your bland, regular hot chocolate." I sipped my drink, already scanning the area for what we should explore next. "Thanks for the drink. And for being a good sport. I know this isn't your thing."

He nodded stiffly, his sharp gaze scanning the crowd like he was in a security detail. In his black leather jacket and jeans, he stood out against the sea of cheerful holiday sweaters like a shadow in the light.

"I think we're safe here," I mumbled. "You can relax."

He gave me a flat look. "Safe? From what? A rogue reindeer?"

It took me a second to catch the joke, but when I did, I burst out laughing, earning a few curious looks from passersby. "Reindeer only run over grandmas, not vampires. Come on. Let's see what's next."

I looped my arm through his and tugged him toward another path. Before we got far, he froze, head snapping to the side like he'd heard something. Without a word, he strode between Santa's Post Office and a gingerbread house.

"Wait!" I hurried after him, confused.

When I caught up, he was crouched in front of a little boy, no older than five, who was crying his heart out. Nicholas's low voice was calm, and after a moment, the boy nodded, hiccupping as he rubbed his eyes.

Nicholas straightened, looking baffled when the kid launched himself at his legs. I gestured for him to pick the boy up. Awkwardly, he did, holding the child like he was made of glass.

"What's your name?" I asked gently.

"Sam," the boy sniffled.

"Okay, Sam. We'll help you find your family. Do you remember where you last saw them?"

He shook his head, fresh tears spilling.

Nicholas sighed. "He said he went looking for reindeer while his sister was looking for fish people."

It took me a second to put it together. "Christmas Under the Sea display. This way."

We walked toward the lake, Sam clinging to Nicholas like a koala. We hadn't walked far when a woman screamed, "Sam!"

"Mommy!" The boy wriggled, and Nicholas set him down just in time for the kid to sprint into his mother's arms.

The father approached us, gratitude written all over his face. "Thank you so much. He just vanished—we were terrified."

"He was looking for reindeer," Nicholas said flatly.

The man grimaced. "Rudolph obsession. I swear, I need a leash for these kids."

"They make them," Nicholas replied, dead serious.

I elbowed him hard. "He's joking. I think!" I assured the father with a nervous laugh. "Merry Christmas!"

As we walked away, I glared at Nicholas. "Leashes are for pets."

He shrugged. "Seemed effective."

I rolled my eyes. "Let's just go. The village is closing soon."

When we reached the Kissing Bridge, a worker stopped us. "Toll to cross," he said, pointing to the mistletoe above.

Nicholas reached for his wallet, but the kid shook his head. "Not money. A kiss."

I barely had time to process that before Nicholas turned to me and pressed his lips to mine.

His kiss was firm and purposeful, but when I softened against him, it deepened. His tongue brushed my lips, coaxing them open, and a heat I hadn't expected flared in my chest. My fingers fisted in his jacket as I melted into him, savoring the sweet, intoxicating taste of him mixed with chocolate and peppermint.

He pulled back too soon, leaving me breathless and dazed.

"Toll paid?" he growled at the stunned worker.

"Y-yeah, dude."

Nicholas strode across the bridge without a backward glance. I followed in silence, my lips tingling and my heart racing.

What the hell just happened?

CHAPTER 5

NICHOLAS

I don't know why I kissed her. I don't buy into those old pagan myths about mistletoe—the whole "you have to kiss the person you're with" nonsense. But after spending the last twenty-four hours stuck with her —her sweet scent, her endless chatter, her off-key singing, and that relentless cheeriness despite being chased by hitmen —I wanted to kiss her.

To shut her up.

That was all it was.

And it worked, for a little while. She'd gone quiet after our bathroom stop and all the way back to the car. Now I missed the sound of her voice. Damn her.

She reached for the car door handle, but I stopped her, my hand covering hers. "Wait. I got you something."

Her eyes widened as I handed her the scarf. Red, green, and white with a Scandinavian pattern—reindeer, snowflakes, and Santas. Not her old one, and definitely not the black and gold one that I knew she hated, but something warm and more festive. More Holly.

"It's not the same as the one you had," I said gruffly, "but it'll keep you warm."

Her fingers brushed the soft knit as she held it to her face. Her eyes shone with unshed tears. "You… you bought me this?"

I shifted, suddenly uncomfortable. "You were in the bathroom, and the gift shop was next door. It was only fair since I ruined your scarf saving your life."

The softness in her gaze evaporated as she scowled at me. "You just had to bring that up, didn't you? You couldn't save my life without destroying my scarf?"

I blinked. "The scarf was killing you. He yanked it and knotted it around your neck. You couldn't breathe."

Her glare didn't waver. "You untangle it, then! My grandmother made that scarf. It was the last thing she knitted for me before she died." Her voice cracked as she turned away, staring at the car.

Regret twisted in my chest, a feeling I'd been growing far too familiar with lately. I laid a hand on her shoulder. "I'm sorry. I didn't know."

She faced me again, blinking back tears. "No. You're right. I'd rather have my life. I just miss her."

"Can it be repaired?"

She laughed softly, the sound thick with emotion. "No. My grandmother tried to teach me to knit, but I never had the patience. I couldn't sit still. Always talking, always moving."

I raised an eyebrow. "I never would've guessed."

She slugged my arm. "Ow. Not nice." Then she shook out her hand, muttering, "Solid as a rock." She dug around in her purse and pulled out something lime green and absurdly fuzzy. "This must be the day for gifts. I snuck out of the bathroom and got you something, too. Ta-da!"

She rose on tiptoes to wrap the monstrosity around my

neck. A Grinch scarf. Complete with faux fur. I held it out, horrified. "What the hell is this?"

She beamed at me. "Now we're both festive. Ready to go?"

Without waiting for my response, she climbed into the car. I followed, still trying to process how she'd managed to make me laugh and cringe in the same breath.

We drove in silence, Christmas music filling the car. She didn't even sing, just hummed now and then. The quiet started to get to me.

"Thank you for the scarf," I said at last. "It was thoughtful."

Her lips quirked in that teasing way of hers. "You were looking cold, Vlad."

"My name is Nicholas."

"Does anyone call you Nick?"

"No."

"Not even your mom?"

I glanced out at the inky blackness of the night. "No one."

She snorted. "It seems so formal. I can't see you as a Nicky, but Nick? Definitely."

After a long pause, I admitted, "My sister called me Nick a few times. She was young and thought like you. My father didn't agree."

Her gaze flicked to me, curiosity sparking in her eyes. "What was her name?"

"Lillian. And no, we never called her Lily," I added wryly. "Even though she hated her name."

"When was the last time you were home?"

I hesitated. "It's been a long time."

"That's not an answer."

I sighed. "Vampires live a long time, Holly. I don't count the years."

She shot me a side-eye. "How old are you?"

"Older than you."

"Obviously."

"I was born in 1910."

The car swerved as she gaped at me. I grabbed the wheel, steadying us. "Careful. Maybe I should've waited to tell you."

Her eyes scanned me, disbelief etched on her face. "You look amazing for a hundred-plus."

"What can I say? I eat healthy and work out."

"That explains why you don't drive."

"I can drive. I just don't like it," I protested.

Her expression turned thoughtful, then her eyes widened. "Wait… do you pick people based on their health? Like, do you know if they're healthy? Is someone unhealthy… bad to drink?"

I stifled a sigh. I should be used to her absurd questions. "Yes, I can tell. I prefer healthy blood. I don't like the effects of alcohol, drugs, or illness. Others don't care."

Her curiosity only deepened. "So you feel the effects of alcohol and drugs? Do you get high?"

"Yes, briefly. Some vampires even keep blood servants for that purpose. It's not my preference."

Her lips pressed into a thin line. "That's… sad. You should help them, not use them."

Her words echoed my own arguments with my father. Humans weren't just food. They were a species we should learn to coexist with. But my father had disagreed, and it had cost me everything.

Her yawn pulled me from my thoughts. I glanced at the horizon, pale light beginning to edge the sky. "We need to stop for the day."

"I made a reservation at a bed-and-breakfast." Her gaze was fixed on the road, and her fingers flexed on the steering wheel.

Something about her careful tone, the way she avoided

looking at me, put me on edge. I narrowed my eyes. "Where are we staying, Holly?"

Holly

𝓘'd spoken to the owner of the Yule House in Little Bethlehem, right on the border of Pennsylvania and New York, a few days ago. They knew Nicholas and I would be arriving early in the morning and promised to leave a light on for us, along with instructions for getting to our room. What I hadn't expected was to be greeted by Mae and Harold Birnham, the owners, waiting for us in their holiday sweaters, smiles bright enough to power the town.

There was only one problem. Well, besides the explosion of Christmas cheer everywhere, which Nicholas looked like he might break out in hives over.

"You only have one room?" I asked, trying to sound casual.

Mae's smile faltered just slightly. "Yes, I'm afraid so. I thought you'd asked for one, and it's all we have left. It's a busy season with the Christmas Marketplace, you know."

Nicholas shot me a glare so pointed I could practically feel it slicing through me. I ignored him. This stop had been my idea. We needed to rest anyway, and the Christmas Village here was magical. It would give him the perfect opportunity to pick out gifts for his family—because there was no way he had anything resembling a present in that black, boring duffel bag of his.

I plastered on my best smile. "That'll be fine, Mrs. Birnham. One room is perfect. You have those shades we talked about, right? My boss is very sensitive to sunlight."

Mae's gaze darted curiously to Nicholas, who gave her one of his trademark blank stares. "Of course, dear. Would you like some breakfast before you settle in? Or I could bring it to your room if you're tired."

"We'd love it in our room, thank you," Nicholas said smoothly, flashing a smile so charming it made Mae blush. I blinked. Where had that Nicholas been hiding?

Harold cleared his throat with a gruff sound, looking vaguely annoyed, but Mae brightened up. "Anything special for you?"

Nicholas leaned in slightly, his smile softening further. "I can already smell the baking—scones, I believe? They smell heavenly. A couple of those, please. Nothing else for me. Holly?"

"Tea and water, along with the food. Thank you so much," I said, doing my best to look calm and not at all flustered by the performance Nicholas had just put on.

Once we were shut inside the room, I exhaled. The place was perfect—a little Christmas wonderland. The king-sized Cherrywood sleigh bed had crisp white sheets and a red-and-green duvet that practically begged me to dive in. The pillows were piled high like clouds, accented with festive plaid ones. There was even a green velvet ottoman at the foot of the bed.

A gas fireplace flickered between two windows, its flame casting a cozy glow on the garland draped over the mantle. Flameless candles flickered softly, and a gorgeous antique gold mirror hung above, making the space feel larger. Heavy, red velvet curtains framed the windows, with blackout shades tucked underneath for Nicholas's unique needs.

Two plush chairs completed the room—one near the window and another by the fire. I could already picture myself curled up with a book, a cup of tea, and one (or three) of those scones. Too bad we were only staying for one night.

"You love this room, don't you?" Nicholas's voice pulled me from my thoughts.

"It's a little slice of heaven," I admitted, my voice dreamy.

"It looks like Christmas threw up in here." He moved past me to inspect the blackout shades like a man on a mission.

I rolled my eyes and closed the door. "I don't know why you hate Christmas so much. It's the most wonderful time of the year—happiness, family, people helping each other…"

He turned, one eyebrow arched. "Really? Says the woman with no family, being chased by hitmen. I'm not sure this qualifies as the most wonderful time of the year for you."

Ouch. That stung more than I cared to admit. "You're right," I said, the joy in the room dimming. "I should be all doom and gloom. Maybe I'll find some sackcloth while I'm at it."

He barked out a laugh. "I don't recommend it. Itchy stuff. Stick to wool sweaters."

A knock interrupted us, and Mae and Harold entered, balancing two trays. They set them on a small table and promised to make sure no one disturbed us before slipping out.

"That's a lot of food for one person," I said, eyeing the trays. "But I'll do my best."

Nicholas gave me a flat look. "What do you mean, for one person?"

"I assumed you don't eat because, well…" I lowered my voice. "You know."

He smirked, leaning back against the chair. "I eat. I just also happen to need blood to survive."

I frowned. "But you haven't eaten anything this whole trip."

"Because your choices are terrible. Pastries, chips, candy. Not exactly nutritious."

I shot him a sugary smile. "Just trying to make sure my blood stays as unappealing as possible to you."

He leaned closer, his voice low and sensual. "Trust me, Holly. Nothing could make your blood unappealing to me. But you have my word—I won't touch you. Unless you ask."

The intensity in his gaze made me freeze, my heart stuttering in my chest, and I felt my nipples tighten. He grinned, breaking the tension, and popped a piece of cinnamon scone into his mouth.

"Delicious," he said with a teasing lilt. "You'd better eat before I finish it all."

CHAPTER 6

NICHOLAS

I groaned as Holly shifted again on the bed. It was a king-sized bed—plenty of space between us—but somehow, her every movement felt like a ripple on the damn ocean. She flopped over to the other side with a dramatic exhale, and just as I started to drift off, she flipped back again.

"Jesus, Holly. Pick a spot and stay there. I'm getting seasick over here."

She froze, the thick duvet clutched in her hands, and peeked over it at me. "How are you even awake? Don't you, like, die during the day?"

I pressed a hand over my eyes. "Where do you get this information about vampires? Television? I'm just as alive as you are—just... different. And I'm serious, your tossing and turning is nauseating."

With a dramatic sigh, she sat up and leaned against the headboard. "I can't sleep."

"Then read a fucking book."

Her eyes scanned the room pointedly. "Oh, sure, because there's a library hidden somewhere in here. I didn't exactly have time to pack a novel, what with, you know, running for my life. And how do you sleep during the day, anyway? Doesn't the light bother you?"

I sighed again, giving up on sleep entirely. "It's natural for me. And the blinds are blackout curtains, so no sun gets in. Think of it like someone working the night shift who sleeps during the day."

She tilted her head, considering that, then nodded. "I guess that makes sense. I'm an early bird myself. I used to get up at three in the morning to start baking, so I'm more of a morning person."

I smirked. "I figured you were. A morning bird, chirping incessantly all day."

Her lips quirked up in a grin. "I don't chirp. Much." She laughed, light and melodic. "Okay, fine. I talk a lot."

"Maybe that's why you're not sleeping," I muttered, unable to stop myself from smirking again.

She rolled onto her side, propping herself up on one elbow to peer down at me. "Tell me more about your family."

I closed my eyes. "No."

"I'll keep talking until you do," she threatened in a sing-song voice.

I cracked one eye open. "I already told you about them. It's your turn. Tell me about your family."

Her expression shifted, the playfulness fading as she flopped onto her back, folding her hands behind her head. "There's nothing to share. Everyone's gone. I'm alone."

Her voice was flat, stripped of the lively energy she usually carried. Against my better judgment, I turned my head to study her. "You mentioned being raised by your grandparents. What was that like?"

A wistful smile touched her lips. "It was wonderful. They lived in this tiny town in western Pennsylvania. My grandma owned a bakery and taught me everything I know about baking. My granddad was a carpenter and had a small farm. It was magical."

Her voice carried a soft, wistful tone, tinged with sadness. I didn't want to ask, but the words slipped out, anyway. "What happened to your parents?"

Her smile faltered. "My dad was a soldier. He died in Afghanistan when I was five. My mom died a few years later. A car accident."

Her voice trembled, sadness threading through the words, and it cut through me in a way I hadn't expected. Even after decades among humans, I'd never grown used to their fragility. Watching them age, break, and die while I stayed the same had worn me down. I'd lost friends, acquaintances—people I let myself care for—until I stopped letting anyone in. I was tired of it. Tired of losing people. Tired of being alone. And somehow, I knew Holly understood that loneliness better than most.

"I'm sorry," I said quietly.

She gave a low laugh, a little watery, betraying the ache she was trying to hide. "Thanks. Do vampires die?"

She wasn't just asking about me. I could hear the weight behind her question. "We're harder to kill than humans, but yes. Accidents, injuries, sunlight—all of those can kill us. We just don't die from natural causes the way you do."

I didn't add the other part, the one vampires don't talk about. Some choose death—stepping into the sunlight when the weight of eternity becomes unbearable. I understood their reasons now, more than I ever thought I would.

She was quiet for a moment, then asked softly, "Why did you leave your family?"

I stared up at the spackled ceiling, memories just as real and painful as when I left. "I didn't leave. I was exiled from my clan."

She rolled over and propped herself up on her elbows,

her eyes wide with shock. "Exiled? Your family kicked you out? What did you do? Drain a human? Break a fang? Scare kids for Halloween?"

I smiled despite her ridiculous comments. "Not exactly. Where do you get these ideas? I disagreed with my father and my cousin, the head of our clan, on vampire and human relations. I wanted us to be more integrated with them, while he wanted us to remain separate."

"But you need humans to survive, right?"

"We have blood servants who serve us during the day and provide nourishment. They tend to pass the role on to their offspring, though some vampires take on humans in the role. Some vampires use other humans too, wiping their minds after they feed."

I waited to see if she would exhibit any fear, but she only looked thoughtful. "Is that how you survived? Wiping human's minds over the years? Or did you bring one of those servants with you?"

I thought about our family's servants. We had a long history with the Fletcher family, with multiple generations linked to our family. "Oliver came with me. He insisted on it. He swore that I would need someone to help me, in case I couldn't find a blood source. At the time, vampires weren't out yet, so my nature had to stay hidden."

"At least you weren't alone." Then she frowned. "What happened to him?"

Guilt still rode me hard about his fate. "Blood servants have a healthier and longer life because of their time with us, but they're not immortal. Another vampire got angry with something I did and targeted him while I slept. They killed him many years ago."

She gasped. "That's terrible. How could that vampire do that?"

I shrugged, even as remembered pain threatened to

swamp me. "It's the old way. Blood servants were fair game in wars between vampires." I glanced at her, hoping I wouldn't scare her away. "Don't worry. I got my vengeance."

She narrowed her eyes at my fierce tone. "Good. He deserved it."

"She," I corrected. "Females can be just as vicious as males in our world. Never forget that, Holly. Vampires are predators. I will keep you safe as best I can. Stay close to me and do exactly as I say until I can get you to safety."

She didn't look at all worried. Instead, she settled into the soft bed, pulling the cotton duvet around her face and snuggling into the pillow. "I trust you, Nicholas. I know you'll keep me safe."

I hoped I could. I was bringing her to my family, to a clan who had little more regard for humans who were not blood servants. They were isolationists, and humans weren't exactly welcome unless they served a purpose. I had to find a way to protect her or send her on her way before we got there.

"Do they know you're coming home?" she asked after a pause.

I sighed. "No."

"Why not? You weren't sure you were actually going to go, were you?"

I grimaced. "Something like that."

A brilliant smile crossed her face. "So you really don't mind all the side trips. It only delays your visit home."

Dammit. She was too perceptive. "I don't like the holidays. I think we could find another way to delay my return."

"I don't understand why you don't want to go home. I mean, I understand the whole being exiled thing. That would put a damper on family reunions. But if I had a family, nothing would keep me from them."

I snorted. "You would think that, but it sucks to be an

outsider, to be the one always looked at as the one who doesn't belong. I have never fit in with them, always questioning and arguing with my father. It got to be uncomfortable, not just for us, but for my mother and sister. It was easier to leave."

"But you didn't leave. You were exiled. That had to hurt." Her soft voice dripped with sympathy, sending me back to the days when I first left.

"I had my pride. I was determined to show them that I was right."

"Pride is a cold bedfellow, or so the saying goes," she said quietly.

"Yeah," I replied. The spackling on the ceiling was really poorly done, unevenly spaced, with the paint worn in spots. But it served its purpose. To distract me from the conversation and the feelings Holly was inspiring in me.

Unfortunately, Holly was not to be deterred. "But if they invited you home, then they must miss you. Do you miss them?"

I thought about my mother and her tears when I left. She had not argued with my father, however, nor had anyone else in the clan. I had been alone. Did I miss them? It had been so long since I had talked with them or allowed myself to get close to anyone. Not since Oliver had died.

She ignored my silence, as Holly often did. I wasn't sure if she hated silence or if this was her way of helping me. "I miss my family, and if I could ever see them again, I would. No matter what. Life is too short for arguments, Nick."

"Nicholas. And you forget, I'm a vampire. I'll live a lot longer than you will." And for some reason, that made me sad. Knowing her light would be extinguished while I would go on. The world would be dimmer without Holly Winters in it.

She stifled a jaw cracking yawn, her eyelids drooping. "On that cheery note, I think I'll try to sleep now."

She leaned over and kissed me on the cheek. "Thanks for the conversation. That helped. Good night. Or is it good day? What do you vampires say to each other when you go to sleep?"

I smothered a smile. "Good night, Holly."

She gave me another bright smile. "Good night, Nick."

And I didn't have the heart to correct her use of my name. It sounded perfect on her lips.

Holly

I woke up wrapped around a warm, firm pillow like a boa constrictor. I was pretty sure I didn't go to sleep with one of those body pillows, and this one was way harder than what I thought those might be. I opened my eyes to a black cotton t-shirt. I slowly lifted my head to see Nick's face smoothed out in sleep. He looked so peaceful, so relaxed, without any of the frequent expressions I was more accustomed to seeing on his face—disgruntled, annoyed, exasperated. All the emotions I was used to seeing from so many people. My grandparents loved me, but I knew that I often tested them. I talked too much. I was too cheerful. I was too eager to please.

Since their death, I'd read any number of self-help books to help me understand my own issues. How could a young girl who lost her parents be so happy all the time? Apparently, I was afraid that I would be a burden, and someone would leave me behind. If I wasn't a problem, maybe they would keep me. Yet somehow, it happened anyway. Sure, they couldn't stop the aging process, so that wasn't their fault. But plenty of other people left on their own. My boyfriend, my bosses, friends. I was always too much. Too needy, too cheery, too everything.

And here I was repeating the same pattern. Forcing my holiday cheer on a vampire who had zero interest in the holidays or me. In fact, I was the complete opposite of everything he would ever want. He had already made it very clear that whatever this was would be a short-term alliance until I got him where he was going. He'd get me to safety, if there was such a thing, and go on his not-so-merry way.

We had an end date that was fast approaching, yet somehow he fascinated me. I could almost feel his pain, his loneliness, and something inside of me desperately wanted to help him, even though I knew it was the worst idea ever. He didn't need or want my help. He only needed me to drive him to his family. I was the one who needed his protection. I needed to stop equating his protection with something more. I think they called it Stockholm Syndrome. I know he didn't kidnap me, but I didn't exactly have a choice about going with him. So it was almost the same thing, right?

As I lay there in the bed, something occurred to me. I never expected a vampire to be warm, almost hot. Weren't they supposed to be cold, like a corpse? Nick would scoff at my idea, especially if I asked him about it. I already knew that he thought I had absurd ideas about vampires, but how would I know any other way? I had never met one, not that I knew of, so I had to ask him. Grandpa always encouraged me to ask questions, even as I was sure he regretted it some days.

The room was pitch dark, so I had no idea what time it was. I felt refreshed, so I suspected it was toward the end of the day. Nick's chest rose and fell in a deep sleep, answering the question of if he died during the day (he did not). But since he was still asleep, I suspected the sun was still up. Or he was more tired than I was.

A heavy weight had settled around my shoulders and down my back, and his hand cupped my butt. I realized not only had I snuggled into Nick, but he had wrapped an arm around me, holding me close. The smaller, cynical part of me wanted to believe that he was just tethering me to him, making sure I didn't go anywhere. The larger, romantic part of me wanted to believe he wanted me, especially the way he gripped my ass. But that way was a path to madness, and I need to suppress those feelings before I got all turned around and started thinking dirty thoughts about my boss.

Of course, I had a leg wrapped around my boss's thigh, his firm muscles pressing against the place that hadn't seen any action beyond the vibrator I had to leave behind when I went on the run. Damn, I had finally found a vibrator that I loved, too. I had named him Chris, for Pine, Evans, and Hemsworth. That wasn't exactly helping me think pure thoughts. I rocked my hips gently, experimentally brushing up against him, and stifled a moan as his thigh hit my hot spot just right. Yeah, somehow, humping my boss probably would not endear me to him at all.

A groan rumbled through his chest like he was in pain, and I froze. "Holly, for the love of all of that's holy, please stop wiggling."

I glanced up to see his eyes staring down at me, a hint of red shining in them. His jaw was clenched, and there were lines furrowed across his brow. His arm had tightened against my ass, holding me in place. Not that I was going anywhere. I slowly began to draw my leg from around his, and he hissed. I stopped all movement and held my breath.

"Sorry. I didn't mean to molest you in your sleep." Okay, so maybe I did a little bit. It had been a while.

He laughed, a raw, hoarse sound, his fingers still gripping my ass. "I think it was mutual."

I knew I should move away, but I didn't want to. Nick was warm, safe, and so freaking sexy. His arm was still around me, the heavy weight a comforting presence. How long had it been since I had slept with a man? Too long, judging by how excited my hormones were just lying next to Nick. Imagine if anything else happened.

"Your eyes are red. Do you need blood?" I asked, almost fearing the answer.

He froze under my touch, then cleared his throat. "I'm fine."

"Then maybe we should get up now," I said reluctantly. I really wanted to linger in bed. I hadn't done that in years. I was always scrambling to get to the bakery in the morning, so if I had anyone in bed with me, I was always the one sneaking out to get to the bakery for the morning shift. More often, it was a cold bed I left behind. But now, with a warm, incredibly sexy body in bed and no bakery to rush off to, well, I wanted to savor the moment, like a delicious cinnamon roll. Only this indulgence wouldn't go straight to my hips.

This one might go for my carotid instead. Though, the thought of him having me as a meal wasn't as big a turnoff as it once was. Maybe once he used me as a juice box, hopefully leaving some of my blood for later, I could persuade him to use that sexy mouth to make a meal of me in a completely different way.

Damn it. When had I ever had such sexy thoughts?

"Do you brainwash humans?"

He glanced at me, startled by my random thought. Or maybe not. He had to be used to my weird ideas by now. "Brainwash? What bizarre new accusation do you have for me now?"

My face burned, and he chuckled. "No, Holly. I don't put those kinds of thoughts in your head. Though I can compel some humans, especially when I need to feed to ensure they don't feel any pain during the process or remember me feeding."

My hand went to my throat and the smooth skin there. He frowned. "I haven't done it to you. I made you a promise."

I dropped my hand. "I didn't think you did."

He arched an eyebrow as if he didn't believe me but said nothing. He lifted his arm and rolled away from me to a sitting position, his back to me. I stared at him, wondering if he was offended or just getting up for the day, or evening, or whatever this was. But his shoulders were slumped like he was tired, and guilt pricked me.

I struggled up to lean on an elbow, and I rested a hand on his back, feeling his muscles bunch under my hand. "I'm sorry. I know you wouldn't do that."

He gave a hoarse, raw laugh. "Never trust a vampire, Holly."

I froze, not knowing how to take his words. I let my hand drop and swung around onto the edge of my side of the bed. "There's an adorable Christmas Marketplace in town where we can do some shopping before we go on our way. You can get some presents for your family if you'd like."

He stood and studied me with a quiet intensity. "What makes you think I need to buy presents? They have everything they need."

I gestured to the beat-up black duffel bag tossed in the corner of the room. "Maybe because that bag couldn't possibly carry presents along with your clothes. And gifts aren't about things people need. It's about giving them something they want that they would not buy for themselves."

He arched that damned eyebrow again, and I swore I

would shave it off if he kept doing it. "Maybe I'm giving them gift certificates."

"For tanning salons?" I retorted.

A ghost of a smile curved his lips. "No, they would be more interested in a Blood-Type Sampler Box, but they were out of stock at the warehouse."

I stared at him for a moment, then burst out laughing. After a moment, Nick joined me, his laugh sounding a bit rusty but warming to a rich, deep sound. "I'm not sure Little Bethlehem has a blood bank with open shopping hours. I didn't see that on their Chamber of Commerce website."

He made a tsking sound. "And we stopped anyway? I'm disappointed in you."

"I was more interested in the handcrafted ornaments and ice-skating rink. I'll look for vampire-friendly things next time. Can you give me a list?"

He flashed some fang. "I'll get back to you on that."

CHAPTER 7

NICHOLAS

I couldn't remember the last time I woke up hard and wanting a woman as much as I had that evening. My fangs had descended, and it took everything inside of me to not roll her on her back, kiss her senseless, and fuck her. I could feel the haze descending upon me, the mating frenzy my father had once discussed with me and my cousin to ensure we were prepared for the possibility, not that he thought it would ever happen for us.

It was rare for vampires to find their true mates. More often, we found a someone with whom we developed feelings and spent many years with, then moved on. Since we lived a long time, vampires often had multiple partners over their long years. Offspring were not guaranteed with every pairing. My father only had two, me and my sister. As far as I knew, he had no other mates or offspring, and he seemed content to remain with my mother, as did she.

I had to wonder if I was feeling the mating frenzy for Holly. My father had not discussed if it was possible to mate with a human. He would have never entertained the notion that it was even possible, but I had been feeling an increasing possessive urge around her, a desire to taste her blood even when I was not hungry, and a reluctance to let her go at the end of the journey.

I sensed something was wrong. I should have been pushing to continue the journey. Pushed Holly to drive longer hours, not stop for inane little side shows. Yet, somehow, I indulged her desire to see tourist traps and holiday frivolity. Maybe it was a reluctance to get home or dread at what I would face at the end of my journey, but either way, I was resigned to spend part of the evening at a Christmas Marketplace, buying gifts for a family I hadn't seen in more decades than Holly had been alive. What would I even buy my family? I didn't know them anymore. But Holly was right. I shouldn't go home empty-handed.

The water shut off in the connected bathroom, and visions of a naked and wet Holly danced through my brain. Who needed sugarplums when I had Holly? She was far sweeter and more desirable than anything else. Damn it. I had to get control of myself, or I'd find myself sinking my teeth and cock into her, sating all of my desires and probably scarring her for life.

"Nick? Are you okay?"

A hand landed on my shoulder, shaking gently, and I whirled around. Holly took a step back, her eyes widening. "I'm sorry. I didn't mean to startle you. You didn't respond when I got out of the bathroom. I wondered if you wanted to use the shower now."

Oh god. How long had I been standing there in a trance? Holly stared at me, clutching an oversized cranberry-colored terry cloth towel to her chest. "I forgot my bag out here. I thought you might want to get in there so we could head out quicker. Your eyes are red again."

Her expression was uncertain, and I cursed myself for scaring her. How could I tell her that it wasn't a sign that I needed blood, but that I wanted her with every fiber of my being? That only her blood would satisfy me? Damn it. She was terrified of me. This was why vampires and humans could never be together.

"It's nothing. I'm just tired."

I moved to go past her, and she reached for me, stopping me. "Nick? Are you sure?"

"It's Nicholas, Holly," I said and continued to the bathroom, closing the door behind me firmly, locking me in with the steam and vanilla and cinnamon scent unique to Holly. My cock hardened even further. At least there was something I could do about that.

Holly

I don't know who shoved a candy cane up Nick—Nicholas's—ass, but I wish it would melt already. When we woke up, he was almost human, and I could forget he was a vampire, something I should be afraid of. He quickly shifted back to his stiff, unpleasant self, and I wondered if it had something to do with his red eyes. He denied it, twice, but I suppose he didn't want to admit he was hungry, not to me, when I had been so adamant that I would never be his juice box. How could I admit that I had had several sexy dreams about him biting me, along with him doing other much more pleasant things to me?

When he got out of the bathroom, he was calmer, and his eyes were their normal dark brown. I didn't think he found someone to bite in there, but what did I know? He followed me without a complaint to the Christmas Marketplace, and I could almost forget his attitude. This place was utter magic. Families were everywhere, enjoying the evening, which was cold with a hint of snow in the air, a perfect night to inspire the feeling of Christmas.

Music echoed through speakers strategically placed along the area, and carolers sang in small groups, dressed in Victorian outfits as they moved among the crowd. Vendors hawked their wares with booths of all kinds of gift items and special things. Not for the first time, I wished I had someone to buy gifts for, but being on the run and short of cash, I needed to reserve it all for my new life. Not to mention the fact that I had no one to buy anything for, anyway.

Reluctantly, I dropped a gorgeous, deep blue cashmere poncho and moved on. Nick—Nicholas—frowned. "Why didn't you buy that poncho? You clearly loved it."

"I also love chocolate and cinnamon rolls too, but I don't eat them all the time either." When he remained standing by the vendor stall, I turned back. "Nick—Nicholas, I don't need it. Not right now. And I need to save my money until I find a new job wherever I'll end up."

I gave him a meaningful look until realization dawned. He dug into his back pocket for his wallet. "I could buy it for you."

My face burned, and I whirled and stalked away. I was tired of being a charity case. It was bad enough that I needed his help to save me from the people chasing me. I didn't want to rely on him for everything, even though it seemed like I was doing that right now.

He hurried to catch up and stopped me. "Are you angry with me?"

I faced him. "I intend to pay you back for your expenses. I'm not a charity case."

He stared at me in confusion. "I never thought you were.

We agreed you would drive me home, and I would take care of all expenses."

"You would protect me and find me a new identity. But I don't want to take advantage."

"A poncho is not taking advantage," he replied, clearly not understanding what I was saying.

I huffed in annoyance. "I don't need it."

"A gift is not about needing. Didn't you tell me that earlier tonight?"

I wrinkled my nose. "You pick a terrible time to start listening to me. Besides, we're just a business relationship." Even if I wanted more. A flash of movement caught my eye. "Come on! There's the ice skating! I want to try it!"

He sighed, and I dragged him along the path, weaving around the families and couples until we stood on the edge of the makeshift rink. The wood railing dug into my palms as I watched the people gliding around the space, some with ease while others falling. Everyone was laughing. This was what I wanted. Fun and joy, something that had been sorely missing in my life for the past few years. And with danger dogging my every step, I wanted to forget about it for a while. Even if I knew it was dumb to pretend it wasn't real.

I grabbed Nick's hand and tugged him to the line for the skates. "Let's rent some skates."

I was surprised that he was such a good sport, and within a few minutes, we were lacing up our rented skates and testing the ice. As I was tentatively feeling my way along the edge, a man glided past way with all the grace of Nathan Chen. Of course, it was Nick, because he just had to be good at this, too.

"Must be nice to have decades to perfect ice skating."

He smirked as he skated backwards by me. "I haven't been on skates since I was a child. Seventy years or so?"

"Asshole," I muttered, and he laughed out loud. If I was

having a better time, I would relish the sound, but I was too annoyed by his ease and skill to relax.

He swept by me again, an arm catching me around the waist and plucking me from the wall, pulling me along with him. I shrieked and grabbed onto to him, but he held me securely.

"Relax, Holly. I won't let you fall."

Slowly, as we circled the rink, I eased my death grip on his arm and relaxed into the motion, skating along with the flow of the crowd and with Nick. It felt almost like dancing, his arm wrapped around my waist, holding me firmly, confidently, ensuring nothing would ever happen to me. Everything faded to the background, until we existed in our own bubble, only the music penetrating our world, as we moved silently, in sync.

But all good things end, and Nick escorted me over to the bench where we reluctantly handed over our skates and stumbled away, adjusting to the much slower pace of walking versus the freedom of gliding. Time was ticking, and I knew we needed to move on.

Then he stopped, his head turning as if hearing something. My heart stuttered, and fear grabbed me. I frantically looked around. "Do you see something? Are they here?"

He held up a hand. "Shhh. Do you hear that song?"

I strained my ears but only heard the chatter of people, the crying of overtired children, and call of vendors hawking their wares. He abruptly shifted direction and dragged me behind him. My legs could barely keep up with his longer strides, but I tried, almost running to maintain his pace.

Finally, he stopped in front of an older man and a small booth filled with handmade, wood boxes. In one, a ballerina danced on a mirror to the sound of a song.

"Is that the song from the Wizard of Oz?"

He nodded, his hand hovering just out of reach from the

box. "'Somewhere Over the Rainbow'. My sister loved that song and the movie. I remember her sneaking out to see the movie, even though our father forbade her from going. She adored that song."

I linked my arm in his, still marveling over the fact that he was old enough to remember when that movie was a new release. "You have to get this for her. She'll love it."

His gaze was firmly fixed on it, but I sensed he wasn't really seeing it. "She's probably moved on now. It's been years."

"And maybe she hasn't. She would love that you remembered something like that."

He nodded, still staring at the box. I caught the older man's eye and gestured at the box. The man smiled and wrapped it in tissue and boxed it up. Nick woke out of his memories, paid the man, and we walked away. As we strolled through the crowd, Nick's hand found mine. And I felt like a teenager with her first crush, already knowing this had gone way beyond infatuation.

I was in serious danger of losing my heart to Nicholas Frost.

CHAPTER 8

NICHOLAS

"What do you mean, we can't leave tonight?"

The innkeepers were not my parents, nor were they any sort of authority figures in my life to dictate what I could or could not do. Yet somehow they were telling me that Holly and I could not leave that night as planned. The only reason we had stopped back at the bed-and-breakfast was because we left the car there while we browsed the marketplace, only a few blocks from the place. It made no sense to drive there.

Mae and Harold, the owners of the Yule House, dressed in new obnoxious holiday sweaters tonight, looked alarmed at my anger and glanced at Holly for reassurance. Holly did not disappoint.

"I'm sure Nick didn't mean to be so abrupt. Could explain what you mean about not leaving? We have to get home for the holidays. I'm sure you understand." Holly laid a hand on my forearm, and I gave them a pained grin.

Judging by their widening eyes, I failed to reassure them. Harold swallowed, the blood pounding harder in his veins, which I could sense easily. "There's a big snowstorm moving in, fueled by lake effect snow from the Great Lakes. We're expecting a few feet of snow and whiteout conditions."

Mae leaned forward. "We were actually very worried about you, thinking you had already left and would be trapped on the highway. It's too dangerous to drive anywhere right now."

Harold nodded. "The state police have asked everyone to stay where they are at least through the night, but most likely through the next couple of days until they can clear the roads."

An icy chill gripped my heart. I wasn't worried about the time. I had a few days before Yule, December twenty-first. Plenty of time to get home. And I didn't think the hitmen on Holly's trail could catch us, since they wouldn't be able to move through the snow either. But I would need to feed soon. And the mating instinct was growing, forcing me to the one woman I needed to avoid, the one woman who had been clear she wanted nothing to do with me in that respect.

Holly glanced at me worriedly. "Where will we stay? I'm sure every place is booked up."

"Do you have a stable we could use?" Judging by the flat look everyone gave me, the joke was not a hit.

"We actually have your room still reserved for you. When I saw the weather report, I made sure to keep it for you, hoping you hadn't left yet."

Holly hugged the older woman. "Thank you so much. That was very kind, wasn't it, Nick?"

I smiled, a much kinder one this time, I hoped. "Yes, thank you for thinking of us. Is there anything we can do to help you prepare?"

Mae eyed me speculatively. "Well, if you wouldn't mind, Harold could use a hand bringing in some more wood for the stove. In case we lose power, it would be nice to have enough wood for the fire. And I can get started on the baking for tomorrow. I expect we'll have people here for more than breakfast."

"Would you like some help? I've been dying to bake some Christmas cookies, and I know how busy you are with preparations."

Mae seized Holly's hands. "I would be delighted. I haven't had time to do tomorrow's baking and would love the help."

Harold clapped his hands. "We all have our orders. Do you need help with your bags from the car?"

I shook my head. "I'll bring them in now, then help with the wood. Point me in the direction of the woodpile."

I watched Holly follow Mae down the hall to the kitchen, both women cheerfully chatting away. Harold shook his head. "They'll be lost in there for hours. I have a bottle of twelve-year-old Scotch we can share when we're done. Avoid the women and any additional chores they have for us. I swear, that woman can invent the most bizarre tasks for me."

I followed him outside, splitting up to grab our things from the car. A few hours later, flakes were falling heavier as we finished stacking wood in the lean-to next to the back door. Harold took off his leather gloves and wiped his forehead.

"Glad we're done with that, and much faster with your help. I don't think you're even winded. I'm much too old for this."

I had heard the way his blood rushed through his veins and did my best to ensure the older man didn't have to take the majority of the loads. I feared his heart wasn't healthy enough for the strain. I ruled him out as a possible blood source, something I had considered briefly since we would be working privately for a while, and I could easily mesmerize the older man and give him time to recover. But it would weaken him too much. I needed to look elsewhere.

I had an inn full of options. Sadly, my body only wanted one person.

We walked into the kitchen, and the smell of cinnamon scones filled the space, along with the underlying scent of Holly, the unique blend of vanilla and sugar cookies that I'd come to associate with her. My blood rushed south, and I hardened instantly. My gums ached as my fangs wanted to descend. I suspected my eyes were turning red, but I couldn't leave without being rude. I faced the large picture window to watch the snow coming down heavily outside.

Holly stepped up next to me, tilting up her face to look outside. "It's beautiful, isn't it?"

I looked down at her, at the smile that curved her lips and the way her eyes shone in the kitchen light. "Yes, it is." She blushed, and I took her hand. "Take a walk with me."

"It's freezing outside," Mae protested.

"We won't be out there long," I said, without taking my eyes off Holly.

Her eyes sparkled. "I'd love to."

Mae sighed. "Well, if you insist, don't go far. Let me get you some gear so you don't get frostbite."

Holly

I don't know what had come over Nick, but a romantic walk in the snow was my catnip. I always loved the first snowfall and had been dying to go outside, but Mae had needed my help, and I missed baking. But we were done, and I was far from tired.

I bundled up in the hat, scarf, gloves, and my coat, feeling more like the Michelin Man than a human, and followed Nick outside. He was barely dressed for the weather, a scarf around his neck and a pair of gloves on, but that was it. He didn't seem affected by the weather, so I wasn't going to ask.

We walked beyond the house, and everything was so quiet, the hush of a night during a snowfall. A few inches had already fallen, and the way the snow was coming down, it would accumulate quickly. I was glad we had stayed and didn't risk the drive. It was almost midnight now, and the sky was so bright from the snow on the ground and the light reflecting from it. It was so quiet that I swore you could hear the snow falling, gently settling on the drifts around us. It felt like we were alone, in a snow globe, with flakes dancing around us and no one else around.

I lifted my face to the sky, closing my eyes, and let the snow fall on me, gathering on my eyes, hair, and skin.

"You love winter."

I opened my eyes and looked at Nick. "I love a nighttime snowfall. It's so peaceful and quiet, like we're the only people who exist. I can forget everything else—all the bad things, everything that's sad—and just be."

He cocked his head as if trying to understand what I meant. Then he nodded. "There are so many people everywhere, always. I suppose snow drives them inside so you can be out here, alone and at peace."

"Exactly. Everyone stays inside, which can be fun too, but it's so clean and fresh. Look at the snow. It's white, pure, not dirty or damaged by shoveling or sand or anything. It's a fresh start. It's beautiful. You lived in New England. You must have experienced snow up there."

He looked thoughtful. "I don't really remember. It's been so long. Snow was just another season for us. We were an isolated community, and snow reinforced that. Since I left,

I've traveled a lot, and some areas didn't have any snow. But I never saw it like this."

I lifted my head again, sticking my tongue out to catch some snowflakes on my tongue. "It's clean, fresh, new. Try it."

Before I could react, he pulled me close and kissed me. His lips were hard against mine, demanding a response, and I eagerly complied, opening my mouth just a little, and he took advantage. His tongue swept inside, cool and insistent, sending shivers down my spine that had nothing to do with the snow falling around us.

Nick's hands gripped my waist, and despite the thick wool of my winter coat, I could feel the strength in his fingers. The knowledge that he could crush me without any effort made my heart race faster, but I wasn't afraid. Not anymore. Not of him. He had shown me his protective side, and I knew that I never had to fear him.

Snowflakes landed on my eyelashes as I tilted my head back, letting him deepen the kiss. His mouth was cooler than a human's would be, but the longer we kissed, the warmer it became, as if my heat was seeping into him. The thought made me press closer, wanting to share more of that warmth.

The snow fell silently around us, muffling all sound except my ragged breathing and the soft growl that rumbled in Nick's chest. The white flakes caught in his dark hair, creating a stunning contrast that made him look otherworldly in the dim light spilling from the bed-and-breakfast's windows. Each crystalline flake that landed on his pale skin refused to melt, as if recognizing him as one of their own—beautiful, cold, eternal.

His right hand slid up my back to tangle in my hair, and he used the grip to angle my head exactly how he wanted it. The possessive gesture sent heat pooling in my belly, and I clutched at his shoulders, my fingers digging into the expensive fabric of his coat. The kiss turned harder, more desperate, and I felt the careful control he usually maintained start to slip.

When his lips left mine to trail down my neck, I gasped. The midnight air was sharp in my lungs, and each exhale formed little clouds between us. I knew what he wanted—what we both wanted—and tilted my head to the side in silent invitation. His chest rumbled again, and I felt the scrape of fangs against my throat, not breaking the skin, but promising what could come.

"Holly," he whispered against my pulse point, his voice rough with need. The sound of my name on his lips made me shiver again. "We should stop."

"I don't want to stop," I breathed, sliding one hand up to the nape of his neck, holding him against my throat. The snow was coming down harder now, creating a white curtain around us, as if we were in our own private world. "I trust you, Nick."

He shuddered against me, placing one last, lingering kiss on my neck before raising his head to look at me. His eyes had gone from their usual gray to a brilliant silver, pupils blown wide with desire. Snowflakes clung to his long eyelashes, and I reached up to brush them away with trembling fingers.

"You shouldn't trust me," he said, leaning into my touch. "I'm not safe."

"Maybe I don't want safe," I replied, letting my fingers trail down his cheek. His skin was cool and smooth as marble, but I knew the fire that burned beneath that controlled exterior. I'd seen glimpses of it, and I wanted more. "Maybe I just want you."

He shuddered under my fingers and rested his forehead against mine. "We should go inside. It's too cold for you out here."

I refused to move, and he looked at me, one eyebrow arched. "Only if continue where we left off."

He sighed. "Holly…"

I pressed my fingers to his lips. "I know what I'm asking for. I want you, Nick, and I'm tired of not having what I want. Please."

As if the word broke through all his reservations, he swept me up into his arms and strode to the inn as if he couldn't wait another second.

CHAPTER 9

NICHOLAS

No one was more surprised when I kissed Holly. I knew she was asking me to taste the snow but, in that moment, I wanted, no, I needed to taste her more than I had ever needed anything else. Then she responded so sweetly, and it was all I could do not to take her right there in the cold, wet snow. Reason fortunately intervened, and I took a step back—only to have Holly pursue me and ask for more. Maybe I was weak, but I couldn't imagine spending another night next to her without knowing what she felt like, how she sounded when she came, and how she tasted.

I'd probably be damned, especially since I knew I had to let her go. But I would deal with that another day. Tonight, I was going to be selfish and indulge in Holly Winter.

I carried her through the now-empty kitchen. The Birnbaums must have gone to bed while we were outside. If I had to get up as early as they did, I'd be in bed early too. Of course, having Holly in my bed would make me spend a lot longer in bed, and I intended to spend all day with her.

I strode up the stairs and down the hall to our room. Harold had brought our luggage while I was stacking the wood, placing it to the side. We wouldn't need it tonight. The fire was crackling in the fireplace, and the bed was thoughtfully turned down. I gently tossed Holly onto the bed, and she bounced, giggling. I tore off my jacket and shirt, tossing it to the side and began unwrapping Holly like the sweetest present I've ever received—her hat, scarf, gloves, and bulky wool coat.

"I always wanted to know what that felt like. I read about it, but never believed anyone could actually do it—"

Her words ended on a squeak as I covered her mouth with mine. The warmth of her lips against my cool ones sent electricity through my long-dead nerves. Even after almost a hundred years, I'd never experienced anything like kissing Holly. Each brush of her lips, each small sound she made, awakened something in me I thought had died long ago.

Her heart was racing. I could hear its rapid flutter and smell the sweet rush of her blood beneath her skin. The predator in me stirred at the sound, but for once, the bloodlust wasn't the strongest hunger I felt. I wanted more than her blood. I wanted all of her.

"Nick," she whispered against my mouth, her fingers tangling in my hair. The sound of my name on her lips made me shudder. Her skin was flushed, warming the air around us, and her scent was intoxicating. The melting snow in her hair released a fresh, clean scent that mingled with her own, creating an aroma uniquely Holly.

I took my time exploring her mouth, memorizing every sensation—the soft press of her tongue against mine, the little sighs she made when I deepened the kiss, the way her hands clutched at my shoulders when I gently caught her bottom lip between my teeth. Every moment with her was precious, every touch a gift I never thought I'd receive again and might never have after tonight.

Her deep pink sweater clung to her curves, and I helped

her out of it, my fingers trailing along her sides as I did so. The silk of her skin was impossibly soft under my touch, and I marveled at the contrast between us—her warm, living flesh against my cool marble exterior. She shivered, but not from cold; I smelled the spike in her arousal, heard the catch in her breath.

I kneaded one perfect breast, the soft flesh fitting perfectly in my hand. I flicked her nipple with my thumb, and she moaned. I tweaked the peak, twisting lightly, and she gasped, her eyes flying open and meeting my gaze.

"There you are. Eyes on me, love."

She flushed, the red spreading up her chest and neck to her face. It was adorable. I unhooked her bra and tugged the straps down and tossed it aside, leaving her bare to my gaze. She laid on the bed, watching me with a small smile on her face.

"See anything you like?"

So many things. Her breasts were perfect, tipped with pale pink nipples, tight and begging for my attention. I trailed kisses down her throat, letting my fangs graze ever so lightly against her pulse point. She gasped, arching into me, and the trust in that gesture nearly undid me. Any other human would have pulled away, would have felt fear at having a vampire's fangs so close to their throat. But not Holly. Never Holly.

"You're not afraid," I murmured against her skin, still marveling at the fact. Her fingers tightened in my hair.

"Never of you," she breathed. "I trust you with my life. With everything I am."

The weight of her trust settled over me like a mantle. I had to be gentle, had to maintain control. My strength could so easily hurt her, but the way she looked at me—like I was a hero rather than monstrous—made me want to prove worthy of that trust.

I kissed my way down to her nipple and sucked it into my mouth, grazing it with my fang, since Holly seemed to like a bite of pain. She dug her fingers into my hair, gripping tightly to hold me in place. I tweaked her other nipple while I licked and sucked this one, then I switched, playing back and forth until she tossed her head, whimpering under the attention.

The sound of her pleasure was the sweetest music I'd heard in centuries—the soft moans, the whispered pleas, the way my name fell from her lips like a prayer. Her nails dug into my scalp with tiny pricks of pain, holding me where she wanted me. I nipped her lightly and lifted my head to watch her lost in the sensation.

She relaxed her hold and explored my body with equal fervor, tracing old scars and the planes of muscle with wondering fingers. The heat of her palms against my cool skin was exquisite torture. I had forgotten what touch felt like in my existence, having spent little time with women, not wanting to risk the chance of exposure or of loss, but Holly was teaching me again, warming me from the outside in.

"You're beautiful," she whispered, her eyes dark with desire as she traced a particularly long scar that ran across my ribs. "Every mark, every scar—they're part of your story. Part of what made you who you are today." Her words pierced something deep inside me, something I thought had calcified long ago. No one had ever looked at my scars—the visible reminders of my violent transformation—with such acceptance, such love.

I captured her hands in mine, bringing them to my lips to kiss her palms, her wrists, feeling her pulse flutter beneath my lips. "You're the beautiful one," I told her, meaning every word.

She was life itself—warm and vibrant and so perfectly

human. The firelight played across her skin, casting her in gold and shadow, and for a moment I wished I could capture this image forever: Holly, her hair spread across the pillow, looking at me with such trust and desire.

When I kissed her again, it was slower, deeper, pouring all the emotions I couldn't express into the gesture. Her hands roamed my back, tracing patterns that felt like they were being branded into my skin. Every touch, every sigh, every whispered word was precious to me. In my long existence, I had never wanted to be gentle more than I did now.

I rolled to the side and shucked my shoes and jeans, leaving me bare. I gave her a moment to absorb the sight and make a decision. She lifted her hips and wiggled, trying to pull off her jeans.

"Damn it," she cursed, frustrated. "How did you do it so effortlessly?"

I chuckled. "Years of practice."

She slapped me on the chest. "Never remind a woman of your other conquests while in bed with her."

I grabbed her hand and held it over my heart so she could feel it beating. "I was no monk, but there weren't that many, Holly. And I never felt about any of them what I feel for you."

She met my gaze, and I saw hope in her eyes. "Really?"

I leaned forward and kissed her. "Really."

I might condemn her if my family ever found out that I loved a human, that my mate was a human, but right now, I didn't care. I'd find a way for us to be together or let her go before my family could find out about her. But I didn't have to think about that tonight.

"I think I love you," she breathed against my lips, and the words hit me like sunlight, warming me to my core. "I know what you are, what this means, and I love you anyway. All of you—the darkness and the light."

I pulled back slightly to look into her eyes, seeing nothing but sincerity there. This remarkable human had somehow wormed her way past all my defenses, all my carefully constructed walls, and made herself at home in whatever was left of my soul. She didn't just accept what I was—she embraced it, embraced me, with a completeness that left me humbled.

"I love you too," I whispered, the words feeling foreign yet right on my tongue. "More than I thought possible. More than I deserve. You've brought me back to life in ways I never thought possible."

She reached up to touch my face, her thumb tracing my bottom lip. "Let me decide what you deserve," she said softly and pulled me down to her again. And in that moment, surrounded by her warmth, her scent, her love, I felt more human than I had in two centuries.

Holly

I couldn't believe I told Nick I loved him. I always told men that too quickly, and they hastily found ways to run as fast as their legs could carry them, usually with some money or valuables of mine in their pockets. But Nick, surprisingly, seemed to return the affection, saying the words and appearing to even mean them. Did I dare believe him?

Then he kissed me again, one of those long, slow, drugging kisses that made me sink into him and just feel. He rolled me onto my back and settled on me, his chest cool to mine, his lips never breaking from my lips. He slid his hand down my side and brushed against the top of my jeans.

"What do you say we get these off of you?" he murmured against my mouth.

I nodded, horribly embarrassed that I couldn't even undress myself in a sexy way. I mean, he just tore off his clothes like some Magic Mike dancer, and I got tangled like a toddler who had never seen clothes before. How sexy was that?

He pulled my jeans off in one easy motion. Seriously. So simple when I couldn't even get them over my ass. Did he rip them? If he did, I would kill him. That was my only pair of jeans.

He placed a kiss on the soft skin of my stomach, and I froze, all thoughts of ripped jeans gone from my brain. He laughed against my skin and trailed kisses along the skin, lower, until he reached the top of my granny panties. Yeah, it had been laundry day when I found the mafia guys in my apartment. All I had clean were my granny panties. How embarrassing.

Nick didn't seem to care that I wore white cotton undies that covered literally everything from the tops of my thighs to my pouch of my stomach. He just ran a finger along the elastic and moved it down, following with light, butterfly kisses that made my stomach quiver.

I watched him with wide eyes as he inched my underwear down, then I felt a sharp pinch at my hip and heard a tearing. "Ooops. I hope you weren't attached to that particular pair of undergarments. I seem to have damaged them."

I scowled at him. "I'm not exactly loaded with extra clothes."

"They were hideous. I'll buy you a hundred more. Or, better yet, wear none."

I rolled my eyes, though I have to admit I hated them, too. "Like we have time for shopping."

"If you can force me to shop for music boxes and snow globes, then we can certainly find time for lingerie."

He spread my legs and settled his broad shoulders between them so I couldn't close them. He then gave me a wicked smile and licked me from my opening to my clit. I gasped and buried my fingers in his hair, the sensation zinging through me like lightning waking up all my nerve endings. He sucked my clit into his mouth and inserted a finger inside, curving it to hit a spot deep inside that made my muscles quiver.

I let my head drop back and simply surrendered to the sensations rolling over me, threatening to overwhelm me with pleasure, and I was more than happy to drown in them. He licked and sucked me like I was his favorite treat, and I could only gasp and moan, clenching his hair, twisting in his hold, but he wouldn't let go far.

My orgasm caught me by surprise, the wave crashing over me and taking me under quickly. When I surfaced, Nick was over me, his hard cock fitted to my entrance.

"Are you ready for me, Holly?"

I cupped his cheek and lifted my hips, wordlessly encouraging him. He slid in, just a bit, and I moaned at the tight fit. He went deeper, slowly, carefully, until he was fully seated, the fit almost uncomfortable, bordering on the edge of pain. I shifted, and he groaned, dropping his head to my forehead.

"Stop moving, Holly. Please. Or this will be over before it's begun."

A laugh burst out of me, and he groaned again. "Sure, you got yours. It's all good for you."

I squeezed around him and moved experimentally. "I'd really like another, if you think you could get on with it."

He lifted his head, an eyebrow arched. "Get on with it? Who have you been with?"

I smiled, having never had so much fun in bed with someone. "Clearly not the right men, since you're the first who has given me an orgasm."

He raised up on his arms. "Let's go for another."

He dragged his cock out of me, and oh my God, the feeling was intense. Then he drove back home, and I believed he could get me there easily. His thrusts were slow and sure, steady and firm, hitting every single spot inside of me, making that wave crest again. I wrapped my arms around him, my fingernails digging into his shoulders as I pleaded for him to move faster, harder.

Nick obliged, moving harder, the slap of wet flesh loud in the room. Again, my orgasm caught me off guard, and I clenched around him, screaming his name. Nick kept moving through my climax, thrusting me into a third one, following me with his own, shouting his own release.

He laid on me for a long moment after, the sweat from our bodies sealing us together. Nick pulled a sheet over us and settled next to me, pulling me to his side. I snuggled against him, my head on his shoulder. I stroked his stomach and the tight striation of muscle outlining his abdomen. I never expected to have my holiday turn into something like this. I had only prayed to stay alive. To find someone like Nick and the connection we had was completely unexpected. But where would we go from here?

CHAPTER 10

NICHOLAS

We fucked several more times that night, my need for Holly bordering on the insatiable. I knew it was the mating bond driving me to build an emotional bond with her, and I tried to keep my distance, but I feared it was too late. It was more than physical between us. I genuinely liked Holly, even the silly questions she asked. She brought joy and light wherever she went. She was the sun to my darkness, brightening my night, and I didn't want to lose her.

Yet, I knew the day was quickly approaching when I would have to make a decision. Remain in exile from my family and stay with Holly, or return to my family and be at peace. I was tired from being on the road, alone, and hiding my nature. I didn't have to hide from Holly, but what kind of life could I offer her in her world? And I knew she would be in danger in mine.

I would have to let her go. Vampires, while technically "out" in the world, were not really accepted and still faced persecution. Alone, I was more at risk, which placed Holly at risk. If I could bring her into the clan with me, she might be safe, but my clan had little use for humans. I couldn't risk her life. I had to let her go.

Dawn was peeking over the horizon. I could feel the sun rising as lethargy seeped into my bones. I didn't need to sleep when the sun rose, but I felt more tired. And, since I needed to feed, I was even more tired than usual. I closed my eyes, settling into the feel of Holly's gentle stroking on my skin.

"You feel cold today," she said, breaking the silence.

I opened my eyes. "What?"

"Every time we've slept together, you've been warm, almost like a furnace. But today, you've been cold." She shifted her body so she could look up at me. "You need to feed, don't you?"

I nodded, unable to deny the truth.

She laid her chin on my chest. "You intended to feed from Harold when you did the wood, didn't you? But you didn't."

I shrugged. "He's older, and his heart is not the best. It wouldn't be good for him if I took his blood, especially with a storm coming. He needed his strength."

She frowned, her brow furrowing. "You fed from the guys who chased us. Didn't you take enough?"

I remembered their blood. It was polluted, and I hadn't wanted to drink more than I had to. I grimaced but explained anyway. "Blood is food for us. Some of it is good, and other is more like fast food. And then there is polluted blood, with drugs or illness. Their blood wasn't very good. It wouldn't sustain me long."

She pondered my words for a moment, while the fire crackled and snapped. "Would my blood be good?"

My gums ached at the innocent question, at what she was unknowingly offering. But I tried to keep an even expression, not betray by eagerness. "Your blood would be a five-course exquisite dining experience."

"Wow, I didn't expect that. I would have thought that

you'd get a sugar high from all the pastries I eat. I'm not exactly into Michelin restaurants or anything fancy."

I hugged her closer. "It's not always what you eat."

In her case, it was what she meant to me. The mating bond meant she was the one person designed to nourish me beyond all others. Her blood would be the sweetest addiction I would ever experience. One taste and I would be ruined for all others. Everyone else would be a pale comparison, if I could stomach drinking from another.

"Then you should drink from me." I opened my mouth, but she rushed on before I could speak. "I need you fully prepared to defend me, and if you're weak from not feeding, then you can't protect me. This is really selfish of me."

I scented her arousal rising, and I knew she meant her words, that she wanted me to feed from her, but it was just a means to an end. She was intrigued by the concept, eager for the experience. Her blood rushed through her veins, and my fangs ached to sink into her flesh, to taste the blood I could scent just under the skin.

She struggled to a sitting position and drew her hair to one side, tilting her head, exposing her neck to me, her body braced for pain. "I'm ready. Let's do this."

Oh fuck. I couldn't resist what was so sweetly offered. I groaned and sat. "Never offer this to another vampire, or you'll find yourself fucked and bitten in that order."

Her eyes widened, and I laughed. "Yeah, I meant it. We'll do this my way."

I took her swollen lips in a gentle kiss. "Thank you for your offering. I promise it won't hurt."

She relaxed minutely. "I trust you, Nick."

This woman. She was too good for me. I pulled her over me until she straddled my lap, my cock trapped between her legs. We leisurely kissed, her arousal growing as our tongues dueled. She tangled her fingers in my hair, pulling me closer and began to rock over my erection, her slick pussy rubbing generously over me. My cock hit her clit every so often, and she gasped as I rubbed against her. I moved a hand between us to tweak her clit, and she began to move more frantically, her moans growing louder.

I lifted her enough to let my cock notch in her entrance, then she settled back down, my cock stretching her until I was fully seated. She began to move, rolling and rising on me, faster and faster, chasing her orgasm. I licked her throat, over her pulse point, tasting the sweat that lingered there and the hint of sweet blood just under the surface. As the flutters of her orgasm began squeezing my cock, I struck, my fangs sinking deep into her carotid artery.

She stiffened at the momentary flash of pain, and her orgasm hit at the same time. She screamed my name, her body clenching around me. My own release exploded, and her blood filled my mouth, the sweetest taste I had never had. I drank deeply, knowing I would be addicted to Holly, not knowing how I would let her go after this.

Finally, Holly slumped against me, her orgasm complete. I licked her neck closed and settled against the headboard, cuddling her against my chest. She drowsily kissed my chest.

"That was amazing. Does it feel that way for everyone?"

"Never."

How could I let her go?

Holly

I relaxed, draped over Nick's chest, completely sated and wrung out. Those last orgasms had done me in. I had expected his bite to hurt, and while there had been a momentary flash of pain when he first sunk his fangs in, it was quickly replaced by a pleasure so intense, I had almost blacked out. I never feared that Nick would get carried away or harm me. Instead, he'd given me more pleasure than I had ever experienced. Now I had to figure out what this meant.

Were we starting something, or was this a one night, convenience kind of thing? He needed to eat, and I was available? Heck, what did I want it to be?

Relationships had always taken a back seat in my life, mostly because I'd been so terrible at them. My schedule was too erratic. I was too busy. And most guys were leeches, always taking advantage. It was easier to be alone, but often lonely. After my grandparents died, I moved from their farm, selling it to pay their medical bills. I didn't miss the town where I'd grown up. I never really felt like I belonged there. Maybe it was being raised by my grandparents, feeling like I had responsibilities, things I had to do that my classmates didn't have. Leaving the town wasn't a big deal. I had no ties once they were gone.

Spending the past few days with Nick had reminded me of what I had been missing, what I hadn't even known I wanted. And I wanted more.

"What are you thinking so deeply about?" His voice was a rumble under my cheek where I rested on his chest.

My hand idly traced a pattern on his very impressive abs, outlining his washboard stomach. "Are you feeling a sugar high from my blood? I ate a lot of cookies last night."

He chuckled. "It doesn't quite work that way."

I propped my chin on his chest. "You said it did for drugs."

"Sugar isn't a drug. Not in the same way as other chemicals. How are you feeling?"

His tone was sharper, his expression intense as he studied me for signs of distress. His concern warmed my heart. It had been so long since someone cared about how I felt. Tears pricked my eyes and blurred my vision.

"Holly? Are you okay?" Alarmed filled his voice, and he sat up, dislodging me.

I struggled to a sitting position. "I'm fine. Just a little tired."

He gripped my shoulders gently and peered into my eyes as if he could read my mind. "Are you sure? Did I take too much from you?"

I laughed. "Take too much? Nick, you blew my mind. I'm going to need to stay in bed to recover all damned day." I shifted on the bed, feeling the soreness between my thighs. "Well, I might need a long bath somewhere in there, too."

He grinned, too satisfied with himself. "I can ask Mae to bring you something to eat to recover your strength."

I rolled my eyes. "I certainly am not walking down there. I don't want to face any of our neighbors after last night."

He leaned back against the headboard, and I settled against him again, sighing and closing my eyes. "What happens next?"

He paused for a long moment. "We check out the weather reports and leave as soon as we can. I'm not convinced your friends aren't hot on your trail. I want to keep moving. Besides, midwinter is in a couple of days."

"Yes, your deadline for getting home."

"My family is expecting me for the holiday, or at least hoping I'll be there."

I twisting my head to look at him. "Hoping or expecting? They know you're coming, right?"

He had the grace to look abashed. "I haven't exactly told them I was on my way. It was a snail-mail letter. I had no time to reach out. At least I'm on my way."

It didn't escape my notice that Nick had avoided the point of my question. So I had to be more direct. "Nick, what happens to us?"

He was silent for so long that I didn't think he was going to respond. Finally, he said, "I don't know."

CHAPTER 11

NICHOLAS

I wanted to avoid Holly's question, and the best way to do that was to distract her with pleasure. But she needed to build up her strength first. And I sensed she wasn't going to let the topic go. Fortunately, another option presented itself when there was a knock at the door.

I swung my legs out of bed, wrapped a blanket around my waist, and strode to the door. Mae Birnbaum stood there with a tray laden with breakfast food, a troubled expression on her face.

"I thought you might need something to eat. Holly mentioned that you would prefer to eat in your rooms this morning."

I knotted the blanket and took the tray, laying it on the table just inside the door. I was about to close it, but Mae didn't appear ready to leave yet. Remembering the manners that Holly was trying to instill in me, I pasted a smile on my face. "Thank you for bringing us something to eat. How is the storm?"

She looked startled. "Oh, there's almost two feet on the

ground already. It's been coming down heavily since midnight. It's not showing any sign of ending."

Dread settled heavy in my stomach, but there was relief. If we couldn't leave, no one else was going anywhere either. But the tension that radiated off the older woman concerned me. "Is everything okay?"

She glanced over her shoulder. "Harold wanted me to leave it alone, but I think you should know. Two men came by last night, while you both were at the Christmas Market. They said they were looking for their sister. She had been taken by her abusive boyfriend, and they wanted to help her. They showed a lot of attention to your car in the parking lot, and they described someone who looked at a lot like Holly."

Holly came up behind me, resting a hand on my back. A chill settled over me, and I knew what I had to do. Anger churned in my stomach, and I struggled to control my temper, knowing I had to keep any signs of my other-ness from showing.

"We appreciate you sharing this with us, Mae. I don't have any brothers, and I can assure you, Nick is anything but abusive," Holly said, her tone strong and confident.

Mae relaxed in that moment, a smile curving her lips. "I know he's not, dear. I was married before Harold, and he was not a nice man. I know an abusive man when I see one, and your man is not like that. But these men, they were bad news. We could tell straight away."

"What did you tell them?" My tone was sharp, and I felt bad, but I needed to know if we had to move immediately.

Holly's hand rubbed my back soothingly, and Mae jerked in surprise. "Oh, we told them that Harold drove the girl to the train station and helped her get a ticket south. He stayed until she got on the train. We're not sure if they believed us, but they left. They hung around outside for a while, but my son came by, and they left. He's an officer in the police department, so they didn't linger for long."

"Why did you help us?"

"Nick," Holly said, a tone of reproach in her voice.

Mae narrowed her gaze at me. "Because I don't think they were good men, and I think you are. Was I wrong?"

How could I answer that? There are many who considered vampires to be monsters, evil creatures who hunted humans. Others worshipped us. Who was right? I shrugged. "I think everyone has a little bit of both in them."

She smiled. "Good answer. I think you'll need a little bit of bad to protect Holly. But I don't think you're mean. I don't think you would hurt someone unless you had to, and that's the difference."

Heavy footsteps came down the hall, and I stiffened, my fangs descending in preparation to fight. Harold came around the corner, his mouth turned down in disapproval. "So, you told them, didn't you? I told you not to interfere."

Mae straightened. "They deserved to know."

"Well, that's it then." He faced me. "What will you do?"

"We'll leave as soon as it's safe." Of course, safety meant sundown and when the storm had passed. Hopefully, those two events coincided.

Harold nodded. "The storm should be winding down by noon. It will take them some time to clear the roads. You might be able to get out tonight. But you can't take your car."

I cursed under my breath. "We'll rent one."

Harold shook his head. "You won't find one anywhere in town. I already checked, assuming you would do that. And I'd bet those men would do the same." He heaved another sigh. "You'll take our truck. It was parked in the garage, out of sight, and they never went near that building. I doubt they know we have one. It should get you through any bad weather and throw them off your tracks."

I couldn't believe they would offer us their truck and put themselves on the line for us. "Why would you do this? These aren't nice men."

Mae smiled sadly. "I told you, I was married before. I barely escaped. Someone helped me once, ensured I was able to get away and not have any trouble. I had a second chance thanks to that Good Samaritan. It's my turn to pay it forward."

Holly leaned around me. "You shouldn't get involved. They could hurt you."

Harold gave a dark laugh. "Let them try. I have a shotgun, and I'm not afraid to use it. Besides, our son and grandson both work for the police department. They're already on alert for these men. We'll be just fine. You take care of yourselves."

"We'll make sure you get your truck back," I assured them.

Harold looked at Holly who was talked with Mae quietly. "You just take care of her and keep her safe. That's what matters."

He moved past me to talk to Holly about his temperamental truck named Lola. I really didn't want to ask why she was named that, because it sounded like a stripper's name to me.

Mae lowered her voice and drew me aside. "I brought extra orange juice for Holly. She'll need it to replenish her energy levels. There should be enough protein there, too. If you need anything else, let me know. I'll prepare a basket for you to take on the road."

Suspicion grew at her words, and I eyed her for a moment. "Thank you, Mae. How did you know we needed extra protein and orange juice?"

She gave a smirk. "Who do you think helped me escape my previous husband? He was the only one who saw what was going on, was the only one strong enough to stand up to the bully." She rested a hand on my cheek. "Why do you think I knew to put black-out curtains on your windows? You're safe here, Nicholas. We'll keep you safe until it's time to leave. Oh, and thanks for not feeding from Harold. I don't think his heart could take it."

Well, I'll be damned. She always knew who I was.

She paused for a moment, as if considering her next words. "Are you taking her to your home, with other vampires?"

I nodded. It was the only way to keep her safe. Besides, the mating bond was forming, and I couldn't imagine living without her.

Mae frowned. "I had hoped you wouldn't say that. Vampires have come a long way since they revealed themselves, but many still don't like humans. Is she safe with your family? Can you trust her with them?"

Mae's words hit me like a stake through the heart. I was being naïve if I thought I could protect Holly. I was a visitor in Grimm Mawr. My father and my cousin, Hugo, who ran the town, had made their feelings about outsider humans perfectly clear long ago. Blood servants were fine. They had ties to the clan, but outsiders were dangerous and to be avoided at all costs, eliminated if they could not be avoided. I had no standing in the clan, and Holly would not be protected, even as my mate. I had to go home. I was tired of being on the road and not being safe, but Holly could not come with me. Until I could find a safe haven for both of us, Holly and I could not be together.

Holly

I had driven pickups in my life. You couldn't live in rural Pennsylvania on a farm without driving one at least once in your life. Heck, I'd learned how to drive on my grandfather's fifteen-year-old Chevy. And I was no stranger to snowstorms either. The roads were messy, but at least there weren't a lot of people driving, so it made it easier to see if anyone was following us.

Snow swirled around the tires as we drove. The roads might have been plowed, but flurries still fell gently and made pretty patterns on the pavement. Plow trucks passed us in either directions, keeping the roads clear and salted, but it appeared most people heeded the advice of the governor and stayed home. Hopefully, the hit men had found a deep hole to hide in for a while.

Nick hadn't said much after the Birnbaums left us that morning. He watched me eat, forcing food on me until my stomach almost burst, while he picked at the food. He didn't want to talk about next steps. He watched the weather reports with a distant expression throughout our breakfast, then bundled me into bed. I expected him to create space between us. The intimacy of the prior evening seemed broken. Yet he climbed in bed and gathered me close, falling into a deep sleep almost immediately. I thought sleep would be elusive, but encased in his arms, warm and cozy, I followed him quickly, only waking when he shook me much later.

I couldn't drive fast with the road conditions, but we didn't encounter much traffic, so that offset the speed issue. Soon, we crossed into New York State, and the traffic remained sparse. We had left the snow far behind, and true night had fallen, leaving us in darkness and silence. Nick was focused on his phone, texting someone periodically, but he dodged my questions about who it was. Dread filled me.

I flipped the radio to a Christmas music station, and Nick flipped it off immediately. I glared at him and turned it back on. He turned it off.

"I can't stand the silence. Either we listen to music, or you start talking."

"It's safer to focus on your driving," he countered.

"The roads are fine. And if we stay in silence much longer, I'm going to fall asleep, and we'll drive right off the road. Not safer," I argued.

He turned his dark eyes on me, looking so remote and cold that I shivered. "Fine. We'll find a place to stop for something to eat."

"That wasn't my point." Where had the sweet and sexy Nick from the previous night gone?

"I need to make a call, anyway."

I shrugged. "You're not driving. Make the call." He gave me a flat look, and I turned back to the road, feeling deflated. "Oh. It's about me."

I had hoped that last night had changed his mind. That maybe he was going to bring me with him to his home, but clearly I had too much baggage for his family. I couldn't really blame him. It was one thing to bring a friend home for the holidays. It was another to bring someone who had mafia hitmen following them. That would be kind of a downer for the festive season.

I cleared my throat. "There's a sign for food and gas up ahead. Do you want to see what they have?"

"Fine."

Wow, showing all kinds of enthusiasm there. "How far are we from your home?"

He looked up. "A few hours."

"That's all? I didn't realize we were so close."

Why hadn't he told me how close we were to his home? If we hadn't stopped at the Christmas Market or the village, we could have been home yesterday. Why didn't he push harder?

He shrugged. "It wasn't important. We had time. And you seemed to want to check out those places."

"They could have caught us. And you could have been home sooner."

I was trying to wrap my brain around why he did something he clearly hated—spending time at the holiday places—instead of pushing me to get on the road. Did he really do them just for me, even though I could have put us at risk?

"I told you that I had time before I had to be home. And I needed time to put your new identity together." His phone dinged, and he glanced up. "Take the next exit. There will be a diner. Luiza's. We'll stop there."

I wasn't sure how I felt about our time together drawing to a close. I changed lanes and watched for anyone following us. "I thought I could maybe join you at your home."

He studied me carefully. "I told you that was a terrible idea."

"But I could stay somewhere nearby, and you could join me later. Maybe?"

He set his phone down on his lap with a sigh. "Holly, I should never have fed from you. I wish it could be different, but we're not meant to be together. It's too dangerous for you in Grimm Mawr."

"You said you have humans there. You have to feed from someone. And you already fed from me and you're not dead yet, so my blood works for you. So why can't I be your blood person or something?"

I was probably being unreasonable, the very definition of a clingy girlfriend, but I wanted to understand why we couldn't work. I had enough men ghost me in the past, and it didn't usually matter. But for some reason, Nick mattered. Damned Stockholm Syndrome.

"It doesn't work that way. Being a blood servant is an inherited position, handed down through generations."

I stopped at the light at the end of the exit and faced him. "What aren't you telling me?"

He let out an exhale. "My family hates humans. You would be in extreme danger if you came home with me."

"More than I'm in now?"

He laughed, a raw, hoarse sound. "Definitely."

Well, crap. That didn't sound good. The light changed and I turned, headed for the brightly lit Luiza's diner. Only a few cars were in the lot. It was close to midnight now. The snowstorm had hit here too, and there were piles of snow around the brightly lit parking lot.

I parked and started to get out, but Nick stopped me. "I'm sorry to hurt your feelings."

Hurt my feelings? We were way beyond that. I blinked to clear the tears stinging my eyes. "I'm fine, Nick. But I need to use the ladies' room, so, if you don't mind?"

He dropped my arm. "Be careful, okay? I'm doing this for your own good. I'm keeping my promise, Holly. I never promised forever."

"Yeah, I know." Of course, back then, I thought that I had no other choices.

Now, I might choose the hitmen. That pain would be over quickly.

CHAPTER 12

NICHOLAS

I followed Holly into the diner. I held her back while I scanned the few patrons seated inside. Mostly truck drivers, plow drivers, and a couple of waitresses who looked bored out of their minds. No hitmen in sight unless they had changed their image, which was doubtful. My contact was also not inside. A flash of headlights combined with my phone vibrating told me that my contact was outside.

"Grab us a table. I'll be right back."

Holly sighed and walked away without looking at me. I immediately felt alone and wanted to pull her close, but I resisted. I had to get accustomed to her being apart from me. It was better this way. She was safer the further she was from me.

I turned and headed back into the cold where I belonged.

My business didn't take long, and I returned to the warmth of the diner. I paused in the doorway until I found her seated at a window booth, sipping a cup of something warm. I thought it might be coffee until she faced me, and I saw a strip of whipped cream on her upper lip. Hot chocolate was definitely more suited for Holly than coffee. She ran her tongue over lip, cleaning it, and I steeled myself against the urge to kiss it away.

I clenched the envelope and wove my way through the maze of tables and booths, sliding across from her.

"Did you order?"

"Only for me. I didn't think they carried O positive."

I stifled a grin. "I prefer O negative personally, which I believe is yours. But French Toast will do for me tonight, with a side of bacon."

She sniffed. "Is that my new identity? Who am I? Daisy Mae Fizzlepop?"

A laugh burst out of me. "I have no idea where you get these ideas. No, you'll be Kate Morgan. Simple, easy to remember."

She frowned. "I don't feel like a Kate. Maybe an Ava? Or a Mia?"

I scowled. She was a Holly, and I hated calling her anything else. "All of your documents are already done for Kate Morgan. We don't have time for you to change them to anything else. By tomorrow, you'll be on your way to your new life in Ithaca. You'll be working as an administrative assistant in a real estate office."

Her frown grew bigger. "Why can't I work as a baker?"

"Because they'll find you that way. You have to change everything so they can't find you."

Tears sprouted in her eyes, and she blinked rapidly to dispel them. "I hadn't realized how much would change. Maybe I should take my chances with the police."

I hardened my voice. "Do you think you would survive if you called the police? Do you think they would believe you?"

She looked out the window, her teeth worrying at her lower lip, not saying anything. I sighed. "I'm going to the bathroom. Order for me if the waitress comes back."

I slid out and headed for the bathroom. When I came back, the booth was empty. The envelope was on the floor, under the table, and a plate of French toast was untouched. I glanced around the diner and didn't see her. Panic rose. I hadn't heard her in the ladies' room.

I saw one of the waitresses leaning on the counter talking to a plow driver. "Did you see my friend?"

"Blondie? Yeah, she walked outside with some guy."

My blood ran cold.

Holly

I studied my hot chocolate, my appetite gone. I couldn't even muster any enthusiasm for the French toast that smelled delicious. I was going to be Kate Morgan, administrative assistant to some real estate person in upstate New York. I'd be alone, with no one I knew. I'd be alone. How long would I be stuck there? Forever? I couldn't live like that.

"What do recommend here?" A man's voice spoke from the booth behind me, and I turned. "Excuse me?"

His eyes were cold, dark. "You haven't touched the French toast, so I assume that isn't good."

I shrugged. "I haven't tried it, so I don't know. This is my first time here."

"It's not like Sweet Crumbs, is it?"

I froze. "Sweet Crumbs?"

"I personally like the sticky buns. Were you responsible for them?"

I was frozen in place, allowing the man to get up and shift

into my booth, pinning me in place. "I think my employer would like to have a word, Miss Winters. Now, follow me nicely outside or we're going to have problems, okay?"

I nodded wordlessly and followed him out of the diner, wondering if this was the last time I would ever see Nick.

The man led me to a black, late model sedan with tinted windows parked in the back of the lot in the shadows. Another man, younger, with dark hair, jeans, and a leather jacket, waited outside, leaning on the car. He straightened when we came out.

"What about the other guy?"

My escort shrugged. "Gone. Let's get out of here before he shows up."

The driver opened the back door, and my escort manhandled me towards it. Then he was gone. The driver gasped and looked around, panicked, for his partner. There was a terrified yell from the bushes just beyond the car that was abruptly cut off. The driver started to shake.

"Get in the fucking car. Now."

He grabbed me and began pulling me, but that yell had shaken me out of my stupor. I struggled, fought for my life, because that was what I was doing. If I got in that car, I was dead. There was no employer that I was talking to. There was no one who wanted to speak with me. They were going to kill me. I knew it. These guys knew it, not matter how pleasant they had made it sound. Nick knew it. I couldn't give it. I could live as Kate Morgan. I could survive.

I kicked out, catching the man in the thigh, just missing between his legs, but it was enough to loosen his hold. "Bitch."

I wrenched free, but this time I wasn't going to run. I didn't know if I could fight, but I was going to try. I was done running. He laughed, a low, sinister sound that sent chills up and down my spine.

"You think you can beat me, little girl? You need your friend, and I don't see him anywhere around."

But I saw Nick. He had risen up from the bushes like an avenging angel, a stream of blood trickling down from one side of his mouth and his eyes gleaming red in the night. He stalked forward, a low growl coming from his throat. I took an involuntary step back, even though I knew he would never hurt me. But he was pissed.

The driver, sensing something or someone was behind him, slowly turned. He saw Nick and, before I could evade him, grabbed me, wrapping an arm around my throat, and pulled me in front of him.

"Back off, buddy, or I'll kill her."

Nick only kept stalking forward, that low growl growing louder, his fangs on full display. The driver dragged me back until we were pinned against the car. "I mean it."

Screw this. I wasn't a damsel in distress. I stomped my foot on his instep, and he howled in pain, his hold loosening. I dropped, throwing him off balance, then rolled away when his hold broke.

Nick took advantage, leaping over the car, grabbing him by the throat, and flinging him over the car and into the bushes where his friend was. He then followed, and I heard a scream, cutoff by a gurgle, then silence.

I dragged myself to my feet and leaned against the car, cataloguing my fresh bruises. Not too bad this time. And I was still alive.

Nick emerged from the bushes, straightened his clothes, and stalked over to me, crowding me into the car. "What the hell were you thinking, coming outside with him?"

"I didn't want him killing anyone inside."

He stared at me for a long moment, a muscle in his jaw ticking as he clenched. Then he pulled me close and kissed me, his lips covering mine in a hard, punishing kiss. My back pressed against the cold metal car as Nick crowded into my space, his tall frame sheltering me from the world that had just tried to hurt me. His eyes, usually a warm amber, had darkened to an almost black gold, and I could feel the tension radiating through his body as he placed one hand beside my head.

"I could have lost you," he whispered, his voice rough with emotion. The words skated across my skin, making me shiver. His other hand came up to cup my cheek, and despite his obvious anger, his touch was achingly gentle. "If I had been just a minute later…"

"But you weren't," I said, reaching up to grasp his wrist. His skin was cool against my palm, a reminder of what he was—what we could never be. "You saved me."

His jaw clenched, and I watched something dangerous flash across his face. "I will always save you," he growled, and then his mouth was on mine.

This wasn't like our other kisses—the sweet, careful ones we'd shared in hidden moments. This was possession, pure and raw. His lips claimed mine with a desperate intensity that made my knees weak, and I clutched at his shoulders to stay upright. One of his hands tangled in my hair, holding me exactly where he wanted me as he deepened the kiss.

I tasted copper and wasn't sure if it was from my split lip or the residual blood from his kill. But it didn't matter. Nothing mattered except the way he was making me feel—safe, wanted, claimed. His body pressed closer, pinning me to the cold metal, and I welcomed his weight, needed it to ground me after the terror of the attack.

When he finally broke the kiss, we were both breathing hard. He rested his forehead against mine, and I felt something wet on my cheeks. I wasn't sure which one of us was crying.

"Nick," I whispered, my voice breaking on his name.

"Shh," he murmured, pressing soft kisses to my temples, my cheeks, the corner of my mouth. Each one felt like a goodbye, and my heart cracked a little more. "Let me have this moment. Let me remember you just like this."

His hands framed my face, thumbs brushing away tears. When he kissed me again, it was slower, but no less intense. I could feel everything he wasn't saying—his love, his regret, his determination to keep me safe, even if it meant walking away. I kissed him back just as fiercely, trying to burn the feeling of his lips into my memory.

When he finally pulled away, his eyes had returned to their usual amber, but they were filled with a sadness that made my chest ache. He took a step back, and the night air rushed in to fill the space where his body had been, leaving me cold and bereft.

"We need to go," he whispered, and I could hear regret and resolution in his words.

CHAPTER 13

NICHOLAS

We drove the last few hours in silence, without even Christmas music to break it. Neither of us wanted to listen to anything cheerful when everything was ending. We were about an hour from Grimm Mawr when I saw the rest area where my contact was meeting us.

"Pull into the next rest stop."

Holly didn't even question me. She changed lanes and drove into the darkened rest stop and parked where I directed her, next to the black SUV. My contact got out of the car, a middle-aged man name Michael Solomon.

I'd known Michael for years. He helped me get IDs when I needed them, along with helping me disappear some humans who needed to find a new place to live. Not unlike Holly. I trusted him, as far as I trusted anyone. Yet a part of me didn't want to hand Holly over to him.

Holly eyed the man from the driver's seat, clear suspicion in her gaze. "So, this is the guy who created Kate Morgan?"

I nodded. "He'll take you to Ithaca and get you settled."

She turned big eyes on me. "You trust him?"

I shrugged negligently. "As much as I trust anyone. He'll be able to contact me if you need anything."

She slumped against the seat. "So that's it. We're done. No contact between us. Everything is through a middleman? Do you hate me that much?"

Tears threatened in her eyes, and I steeled myself against them. "We discussed this. It's safer for you to go with Michael."

"Will I see you again?" Her voice was small, tentative, and my gut clenched.

That was the question. I was going home, uncertain of my welcome. Sure, my mother had invited me, but I didn't know if my father or cousin even knew I was coming. I was technically still under exile, so I might not have a place to stay beyond Yule. But if I could stay, I needed the break Grimm Mawr offered. I was tired of being alone. And maybe I could eventually bring Holly there with me. Ithaca wasn't that far away. I could visit her, make sure she was okay, and, once everything has settled, we could be together. If she still wanted me.

"Of course you will. For now, I need you to be safe. Michael will help you."

She stared out the front window, her fingers still clenching the steering wheel. Then she eased her grip and balled them in her lap. "Fine. But don't expect me to be waiting for you."

We got out of the car and joined the balding, older man leaning against his car. He gave me a quick nod. "Heard you ran into trouble at the diner."

"We handled it."

"They won't stop. A new identity won't be enough."

I was aware of that. I had already put steps in place to manage the mafia boss who had put the hit out, reaching out to a few contacts who were already moving in. "I'll handle it."

Michael studied me for a moment while Holly's wide gaze darted between us. "What does this mean?"

"It means that you need to listen to everything Michael tells you, Kate," I said firmly.

She wrinkled her nose. "I still don't like that name."

Michael grinned. "Sorry. I only had so many options on hand." He glanced at me. "Are you ready to leave?"

She sighed and looked at me. "I guess?"

I jerked my chin to Michael, who stepped away, giving us some semblance of privacy. I pulled Holly close. "I'm sorry that it couldn't be any different. But this really is for the best."

She tilted her head. "For whom? For you? Someday, you'll realize what you lost, and you'll be all alone. You need to open yourself up, Nick. You're not tired from being on the road. You're tired from being alone. You could have been with someone who loves you. Instead, you chose to protect yourself and retreat."

She turned away, then paused. "I hope you don't regret it someday."

She walked towards Michael, who opened the passenger door. "Can I pick the music?"

"Only if you like Christmas music."

"Perfect." The sound of musical laughter echoed in the empty parking lot, then was cut off as the door closed.

Michael looked at me. "I'll keep her safe, Nicholas."

I nodded. "I know you will."

He got in the car and drove off, leaving me in the dark and cold. I had never noticed how alone I was before Holly. I already missed her.

Holly

. . .

The night air bit at my exposed skin as Michael guided me toward his car, his hand gentle but firm on my elbow. I let him lead me, too numb to resist, my mind replaying Nicholas's last words over and over: "You need to go. It's not safe." The way he'd turned away from me, shoulders rigid, refusing to meet my eyes—it felt like a physical wound in my chest.

Michael opened the passenger door for me, and I slid in without a word. The leather seat was cold against my back, and I wrapped my arms around myself, trying to hold in whatever warmth I could find. I heard him get in on the driver's side, but he didn't start the car immediately.

"He's trying to protect you," Michael said softly, his hands resting on the steering wheel. "Even if he's doing it in the most emotionally stunted way possible."

I let out a bitter laugh that sounded more like a sob. "By pushing me away? By pretending what we have means nothing?" I pressed my fingers to my lips, trying to hold back the tears that threatened to spill. "You didn't see his face. He looked right through me, like the last few days never happened."

Michael turned in his seat to face me. In the dim light from the streetlamp, his expression was gentle but serious. "Holly, you need to understand something about Nicholas. Before you, he hadn't let anyone—human or vampire—get close to him in decades. The walls he built around himself were legendary, even among his kind."

"Then why?" My voice cracked. "Why let me in at all if he was just going to—"

"Because you crashed through those walls without even trying," Michael interrupted. "You didn't see him before you came into his life. He was existing, not living. Going through the motions. Then suddenly there was this human woman who wasn't afraid of him, who challenged him, who made him laugh for the first time in years."

I stared out the windshield, watching as a light snow began to fall, flakes catching the glow of the streetlamps. "He's going back to them, isn't he? His family?"

Michael nodded slowly. "He needs to face them, Holly. What happened when he was turned—it left scars deeper than any of us realized at the time. His father's rejection, his mother's silence, his sister turning her backs on him... He was twenty-five and suddenly completely alone in a world he didn't understand."

"But that was over a century ago," I whispered.

"Some wounds don't heal with time alone," Michael explained. "Especially when you never let yourself acknowledge them. Nicholas has spent the last hundred years convincing himself he doesn't need anyone, that being alone is safer. Then you came along and showed him what he's been missing, and it terrified him."

I turned to look at Michael, tears finally spilling over. "I would have gone with him. I would have stood by him while he faced them."

"I know you would have," Michael said, reaching over to squeeze my hand. "And that's exactly why he couldn't let you. He's convinced himself that everyone he loves eventually leaves him. His family taught him that lesson, and he's never unlearned it. The thought of you seeing him vulnerable, seeing him possibly rejected by them again—"

"So instead, he rejects me first?" I pulled my hand away, anger finally breaking through the numbness. "How is that fair?"

"It's not," Michael agreed. "But Holly, the fact that he's

going back at all? That's because of you. You showed him that connecting with people doesn't always end in pain. You made him want to try to heal those old wounds." He paused, studying my face. "And the fact that he's pushing you away to keep you safe, rather than letting you walk into a potentially dangerous situation with his family? That's love, even if he can't admit it to himself yet."

I closed my eyes, letting my head fall back against the headrest. "I hate that I understand what you're saying. I hate that it makes sense. I hate that I still love him, even when he's breaking my heart."

"He'll come back," Michael said with quiet certainty. "Once he faces his demons, once he realizes that being alone isn't actually keeping anyone safe—he'll come back to you. You're the first person in a century who's made him feel human again."

The snow was falling harder now, floating on the windshield. I watched the flakes settle on the glass, melting from the heat and creating trails of water. "And what am I supposed to do until then?"

"You let me take you somewhere safe," Michael said, finally starting the car. "You let yourself be angry with him, and sad, and whatever else you need to feel. And you remember that sometimes love means giving someone the space they need to heal, even when it hurts."

I nodded, not trusting myself to speak. As Michael pulled away from the curb, I pressed my forehead against the cool glass of the window. Somewhere in the darkness, Nicholas was heading toward his past, toward the family that had abandoned him. Part of me wanted to hate him for not letting me be there for him, but Michael's words echoed in my mind. A century of isolation, of believing love only led to pain—it wouldn't be undone in only a few days or weeks, no matter how intense our connection.

"Tell me about them," I said finally, my breath fogging the window. "His family. Tell me what he's walking into."

Michael glanced at me, a small smile touching his lips. "There you go. Always trying to understand, even when he's making it impossibly difficult."

CHAPTER 14

NICHOLAS

I'd forgotten how the mountains looked at night, their silhouettes black against the star-strewn sky. The familiar winding road felt both eternal and too short as my headlights carved through the darkness and the swirling snow. Somewhere behind me, Holly was probably crying in Michael's car, and the thought made my hands tighten on the steering wheel until the leather creaked.

I almost missed the moment I crossed into Grimm Mawr. There was no thunderous magical barrier, no crushing weight of ancient wards—just a subtle shift in the air, like stepping from one room into another. The "Welcome to Grimm Mawr" sign gleamed under my headlights, its fresh paint a far cry from the weathered marker I remembered. The population number listed below made me blink: 15,000. It had been barely 3,000 when I left.

As I crested the final hill, I had to pull over. The town spread out below me, a constellation of lights that rivaled the stars above. Holiday decorations sparkled everywhere—wrapped around lamp posts, strung between buildings, twinkling in shop windows. And there were people. So many people, strolling along the sidewalks despite the late hour, their laughter carrying on the crisp December air. Humans alongside supernaturals, I realized with a start. Humans walking freely through what had once been strictly supernatural territory.

I forced myself to start driving again, navigating streets that were both familiar and strange. The old bookshop where I'd spent countless hours was now a bustling café, its windows steamy and warm. The town square had been transformed into a holiday market, wooden stalls selling everything from hot chocolate to handmade crafts. A group of teenagers—some warm-blooded, some not—huddled around a fire pit, sharing marshmallows and stories.

I couldn't help but think how Holly would have been utterly charmed by the sight.

"What happened here?" I murmured to myself, turning onto the long drive that led to my family's estate. The gravel path was now paved, lined with elegant streetlamps that cast a gentle glow through the ancient oaks. And there, at the end, stood my childhood home.

The mansion I remembered had been imposing, deliberately intimidating, with its dark stone and gothic architecture. Now, soft white lights outlined every window, wreaths hung on every door, and warm, yellow light spilled onto the snow from within. It looked… welcoming. Like somewhere Holly would have loved.

The thought of her hit me like a physical blow. I'd been so certain I was protecting her, so convinced that bringing her here would put her in danger. But this place, this transformed version of my hometown, wasn't the fortress of darkness and danger I'd described to Michael.

I'd barely put the car in park when the front door flew open. A figure burst out—my mother, moving faster than I'd seen her move in decades. Before I could even get out of the car, she was there, yanking my door open.

"Nicholas?" Her voice broke on my name. "Oh, my darling boy—"

I found myself wrapped in an embrace that smelled of jasmine and home, her fingers clutching at my coat like she was afraid I'd disappear. Over her shoulder, I saw my father approaching more slowly, but his face—I'd never seen him look so openly emotional.

"You're home," he said simply when he reached us. "You're safe."

"I..." The words stuck in my throat. A century of rehearsed accusations and bitter speeches crumbled in the face of their genuine joy at seeing me. "What happened here? The town, the humans—"

My mother finally released me, though she kept one hand on my arm as if maintaining contact was essential. "Come inside, darling. You must be exhausted from driving. We have so much to tell you."

The entrance hall was exactly as I remembered, but warmer somehow. Family photos lined the walls—recent ones, I realized, of my sister and her children, of town events and holiday gatherings. I had missed so much. Lillian as a mother. I couldn't even fathom that.

"We changed with the times," my father explained as he led us to the sitting room. "About twenty years ago, we realized we couldn't keep living in isolation. The world was changing too quickly. Your cousin Hugo went into his long sleep thirty years ago, and it was something of a wake-up call. The old ways weren't sustainable."

"The barriers?" I asked, sinking into my old favorite armchair. It had been reupholstered in a rich burgundy.

"Modified," my mother said, perching on the sofa beside me.

"They still keep out those who mean harm, but they welcome those who would be friends. We have a council now—humans and supernaturals of all species working together. The holiday market was their idea." She smiled fondly. "The children love it. And you should see Halloween. It's an entire month now."

"Children?" I echoed.

"Human and supernatural children growing up together," my father confirmed. "It's been… enlightening. Challenging sometimes but rewarding. We've learned so much. It was what you often said. We could learn to live together if we only tried. There have been some bumps along the way, but overall, it has been wonderful."

I closed my eyes, thinking of Holly's face when I'd told her she couldn't come with me, that it wasn't safe. How many times had she told me I was stuck in the past? How many times had she insisted that things could change, that people could change? I had become what I had accused my family of —stuck in the past, mired to the old ways, and hadn't even give Holly a chance. She had won me over, and I sent her away.

"Nicholas?" My mother's voice was gentle. "Are you alright?"

"I made a terrible mistake," I whispered. "There's someone I left someone behind because I thought it wasn't safe for her here. I thought you wouldn't welcome her."

"At one time, we might not have welcomed her. But now… Bring her," my father said immediately. "Whoever she is, bring her home."

Home. The word echoed in my chest, filling empty spaces I'd forgotten existed. I looked around at the warm room, at my parents' concerned faces, at the evidence of decades of change and growth I'd missed because I'd been too afraid to look back.

"I need to go," I said, standing abruptly. "I need to find her."

My mother smiled knowingly. "We understand. And Nicholas? We've missed you. Every day."

As I strode out the door to my car, my phone already in hand, I realized that Holly had been right about something else too—sometimes love meant taking chances, even when you were afraid. Especially when you were afraid.

Holly

Michael pulled off at a run-down diner off the highway in Oneota. I was feeling a bit gun shy about stopping anyway, especially a place that had seen better days, or even years in this case. It seemed they were magnets for hitmen these days, but my bladder was screaming at me, and my eyes were gritty from crying, so I could use the ladies' room and freshen up. I wasn't hungry, so it surprised me to come out of the bathroom to find Michael seated in a booth, studying the laminated menu.

I slid into the vinyl seat across from him. "I thought you wanted to get to our destination before more snow hit."

He nodded noncommittally. "We have time for something to eat. This diner has an excellent reputation for burgers."

I glanced around in disbelief. The fluorescent lights flickered overhead, casting an intermittent sickly glow across the cracked vinyl booths that had been patched with duct tape that no longer matched the burgundy vinyl. I traced my finger along a deep groove in the Formica tabletop, wondering how many decades of coffee cups and restless hands had left their mark here. The window beside me was grimy, streaked with what looked like years of half-hearted cleaning attempts, but through it, I could see the neon "OPEN" sign reflecting off the wet pavement outside.

The menu in front of me was sticky, its laminated pages curling at the corners, food stains creating a kind of abstract art around the prices that had been crossed out and rewritten multiple times in different colored pens. A lonely piece of pie rotated slowly in a dusty display case, its meringue peaks looking more like plastic than food.

Michael had promised to take me somewhere safe. I supposed this qualified—it was hard to imagine anyone, vampire or human, looking for me in a place that time itself seemed to have forgotten.

"Is it safe?" I whispered.

He glanced at me. "You're being chased by hitmen, and you're worried about a diner?"

"It seems silly to survive the mafia only to be killed by salmonella."

"Honey, you won't get that here. Dominick cooks everything until it's shoe leather. Salmonella can't survive that. Now I can't say much about that Noro virus. Iris isn't much for cleaning like she should," said the waitress in the bubblegum pink polyester uniform, platinum bouffant, and more makeup than I'd seen since the Drag Queen Bingo show I went to in Pittsburgh.

That did not reassure me. I set the menu down. "Coffee. Black."

Michael grunted. "Cheeseburger. Well done, with a side of onion rings."

I waited for her to leave and leaned forward. "Don't you think we should get moving?"

"Not yet. We have time."

He was avoiding my gaze, reading that menu like it was

the most absorbing, fascinating novel of all time. I narrowed my gaze, suspicion growing. "What are you waiting for?"

He lifted his head and arched an eyebrow. "Waiting? For my dinner, of course. Nicholas dragged my ass out of bed to escort you to your new home. I didn't have time for dinner. I think I deserve something to eat."

His words rang true, but something was off. But I couldn't find it inside of me to care. Not anymore.

I stared into my coffee, watching the fluorescent lights create oil-slick rainbows on its surface, when I heard the bell above the door chime. I didn't look up—I'd stopped looking up a few patrons ago, tired of the disappointment when it wasn't him. The squeaking of shoes on linoleum told me someone was approaching, and I tensed when they stopped at my booth.

"Your coffee looks cold."

My heart stuttered in my chest. I knew that voice. Slowly, I raised my eyes to find Nicholas standing there, looking somehow both perfectly put together and completely wrung out. His dark hair was windswept, his normally impeccable clothes slightly rumpled, and his eyes—God, his eyes were fixed on me like I was water and he'd been wandering in the desert.

He loomed over us, his gaze almost eating me up, then he shot Michael a thoroughly put out glare. "This is the place you stopped? You could have picked up a deadly disease eating here."

"That's what I said," I chirped before remembering I was pissed off at him.

Michael shrugged, then slid out of the booth, throwing down a twenty. "It wasn't this bad the last time I was here. But that was twenty years ago, I think. Hard to remember. If you were that concerned, maybe you shouldn't have walked away, brother."

"Maybe you should handle that other situation we talked about," Nick snarled.

Michael only smiled. "Now that you got your head out of your ass, I'll head south and make sure no one bothers sweet Holly again." He turned to me and took my hand, kissing the back of it. "It's been a pleasure and if Nicholas is any kind of asshole, call me. I'd be happy to take care of you."

Nick growled, and Michael dropped my hand, chuckling. He headed for the door. "I'll take care of your problem, Holly. And remember, sometimes it's hard to take a chance. Be brave. Merry Christmas."

And he ambled out of the diner with a wave to the waitress, who barely noticed he was gone.

I narrowed my gaze at Nick as he took my hand. "Is he a vampire, too?"

"A damned nosy asshole, but yes, he is," Nick muttered. "I can't believe he stopped here. Endangering your life like this. Come on. We're leaving."

He tugged my hand, but I had had enough of being dragged places. I yanked my hand back and folded my arms across my chest. "I don't think so. I'm tired of being told what to do. You dumped me, Nick. You didn't even ask me."

To my horror, tears pricked my eyes. I hated that I was crying when all I wanted to do was yell and scream and throw things. Why couldn't I have the big angry scene and scare everyone? No, I had to go and cry and be a baby.

I stared at the table, tears blurring my vision. A handkerchief appeared, and I hesitated. "It's cleaner than the napkins here."

Nick slid into the booth across from me with a heavy sigh. "I made a mistake, okay? I knew as soon as you left, but I had convinced myself that I was protecting you."

"You were protecting yourself," I corrected sullenly.

He gave a nod. "You're right. I was. I convinced myself

that no one would accept you in my hometown and never even gave it a chance. Yet, I didn't take one thing into consideration. You."

I lifted my head and met his gaze, hope kindling in my soul. His eyes were burning into me, filled with passion and something else I dared not define.

"You are pure light and joy, Holly. I was empty, drained of everything when I headed for home. I was retreating, feeling like I had nothing left when I met you. You brought light, joy, and laughter into my life, even when I didn't want it. You dragged me, kicking and screaming, into the holiday season and made me live again. If you could do that for me, you could make anyone love you. After all, you made me fall in love with you."

My jaw fell open, and I stared at him, not daring to believe what I was hearing. "In love?"

He reached out and took my hands. "Yes, Holly. I love you. Leaving you was the single hardest thing I ever had to do, and I did it because I was afraid. I thought if you came with me, you would realize that life with me was too hard, too confining for your light, and you would leave me. But I can't live without you."

"What about what I want? You never asked me. You just made assumptions about what I want for myself."

He froze, his expression growing still. "You're right. This is not about me, but about you and what you want. I won't force you to do anything you don't want."

I pulled my hands back, already regretting the lack of contact. "So, if I want to leave and go my own way, you'll let me? Even if I want to go back home?"

He sucked in a deep breath, then nodded. "Michael is on his way there to handle your problem as we speak. You will be safe. I promise you."

I studied him for a long moment, watching as he struggled to contain himself. "What if I want to go to Grimm Mawr and kick your father's ass for kicking you out?"

Hope flared in his eyes, and one corner of his lip curved up. "I would gladly drive you, but I feel I should point out that he has welcomed me home and strongly suggested that I bring you back with me. Grimm Mawr has changed. It's not the same town it used to be."

Disappointment pricked the balloon of happiness that had been growing inside of me. "So that's why you're here? It's now okay to have me back there?"

"No, I was coming for you, anyway. I knew I could never be happy living without you. But now we have a place where we can live together, openly, and not worry about anything."

His open and earnest expression was so opposite to everything I had seen from him to this point. He had been so remote and closed off except during select times in our journey. But now, I felt like I was seeing the real Nick. Could I trust that he really wanted me? What had Michael said? Be brave. He wasn't wrong. I had lived my life on the move, never getting close to anyone for a long time since my grandparents had died, never trusting that anyone would stick around. Nick's life had been so very similar. He was offering me a home, a place to belong, by his side. And I already knew I was in love with him and would never love another. Would I let pride get in the way of my happiness?

The waitress dropped a plate with a well-done burger and a side of onion rings on the table in front of us. "Will there be anything else?"

We both stared at the unappealing meal and shook our heads. I reached for Nick's hands. "We have to be going home now. Thanks!"

I slid out of the booth, dragging him with me. He pulled me into his arms. When his lips met mine, the entire world faded away—the dank diner, the cracked vinyl, the waitress popping her gum. There was only Nicholas, his cool lips moving against mine with infinite tenderness, his hand sliding into my hair as he deepened the kiss. I clutched at his shirt, pressing closer, and felt him smile against my mouth.

When he finally pulled back, just far enough to rest his forehead against mine, his breath was uneven. "Let's go home," he whispered.

"Home?" I echoed, my fingers still twisted in his shirt.

He kissed me again, soft and quick. "Home. To our ridiculous, magical, changing town. To my family who already loves you because you brought me back to them. To wherever you are, because that's home now."

The ancient linoleum creaked under our feet as I pushed up on my toes to kiss him one more time. "Take me home, then."

EPILOGUE

NICHOLAS

I watched Holly's face as she took in the grand Christmas tree in our family's parlor, her eyes reflecting the hundreds of tiny white lights that twinkled among the antique ornaments. Some of those delicate glass baubles were older than I was, carefully preserved through generations. Now they shared branches with newer additions—including the handmade ornament Holly had bought at one of the Christmas markets on our journey, a delicate silver snowflake that caught the light perfectly.

"Your sister's children are adorable," Holly whispered to me, nodding toward where my nieces and nephews were sprawled on the Persian rug, playing some complicated card game that seemed to involve a lot of giggling. Their parents —my sister Lillian and her husband Marcus—sat nearby on the velvet settee, taking turns dealing cards into the game.

"They're cheating, you know," I murmured back, wrapping my arm around her waist and pulling her into my lap. "Vampire hearing. They can tell when the kids are bluffing."

Holly stifled a laugh against my shoulder. "And you're not going to call them out on it?"

"And risk Lillian's wrath on Christmas? I may be immortal, but I'm not stupid."

From her spot by the fireplace, my mother caught my eye and smiled knowingly. She was wearing the cashmere sweater Holly had helped me pick out, its deep burgundy color perfect against her pale skin. The sight of her, contentedly knitting what looked like another scarf for her ever-growing collection of grandchildren, made something in my chest tighten. How many Christmases had I missed, thinking I wasn't welcome here?

"Penny for your thoughts?" Holly squeezed my hand, and I realized I'd been lost in memory.

"Just thinking about how right you were," I admitted quietly. "About everything."

"I enjoy hearing that," she teased.

A burst of laughter drew our attention to the entrance hall, where my father was returning from the kitchen with a tray of hot chocolate—regular for the humans, and blood-warmed for the vampires. The sight of him, this ancient and powerful vampire, carefully balancing marshmallows and candy canes, was something I was still getting used to.

"Holly," he called out, "I believe I promised to show you the family photo albums. Would you like to see just how unfashionable Nicholas was in the 1920s?"

I couldn't believe how well my father had taken to Holly and she to him. They spent hours together, talking and laughing. And with my mother, she was trying to learn how to knit, with a modicum of success. What Holly didn't know was under the tree was her repaired scarf. My mother had salvaged it, with a few adjustments. And Lillian and the kids were fascinated by Holly's baking skills. Holly was already looking for a storefront in town for her bakery. She had fit in like the puzzle piece we were always missing but never knew was gone.

"Father," I groaned, but Holly was already pulling me toward the leather armchair where he was settling with the albums.

"Oh, absolutely," she said, perching on the armrest beside me as I sat. "I bet he tried to rock the Oxford bags look."

"The what?" one of my nieces asked, abandoning the card game to join us.

"Wide-legged trousers," my father explained, opening the first album. "Your Uncle Nicholas thought they made him look sophisticated."

"They did," I protested, but my words were drowned out by Holly's delighted gasp as my father revealed the first page of photographs.

"Oh my God, look at your hair!' She pointed to a sepia-toned image of me looking particularly brooding against a garden wall. "How much pomade did you use?"

"A gentleman never reveals his secrets," I said with as much dignity as I could muster, but I couldn't help smiling as more of my family gathered around to look at the photos.

The evening passed in a warm blur of stories and laughter. Lillian's youngest discovered she could balance a candy cane on her nose, leading to an impromptu competition that even my mother joined in on. Margaret's twins convinced Holly to teach them some modern dance moves, which quickly devolved into all of us attempting to learn what Holly called "the floss." I was certain there were now several incriminating videos of that particular endeavor saved on various phones.

As midnight approached, I found myself by the window, watching snow begin to fall in the garden. Holly was curled up on the sofa, deep in conversation with my sisters about some television show they all watched. The sight of her there, so perfectly at ease among my family, made me wonder how I could have ever thought this wouldn't work.

"She fits, doesn't she?" My mother's voice was soft as she joined me at the window. "Like she was always meant to be here."

"I almost lost her," I admitted. "Because I was too afraid to believe things could change. Because I was too afraid to take a chance."

"But you didn't lose her," my mother reminded me, patting my cheek in that way she had when I was small. "You found your way back. Both to her and to us."

A peal of laughter drew our attention back to the room—Holly was now teaching my father some complicated hand-clapping game, his usual gravity forgotten as he concentrated on getting the pattern right. My sister and her husband were calling out unhelpful advice, while the children cheered them on.

"I don't deserve this," I whispered.

"Love isn't about deserving, darling," my mother said. "It's about accepting. And you've finally learned to do that."

Holly looked up then, catching my eye across the room. Her smile was radiant as she held out her hand to me. "Nick! Come help me teach them 'Miss Mary Mack!'"

As I crossed the room to join them, I realized my mother was right. This—all of this—wasn't about deserving. It was about opening your heart and letting love in, whether it came in the form of family reconciliation, or a human woman brave enough to love a vampire, or the simple joy of teaching ancient vampires playground games on Christmas night.

"I love you," I whispered in Holly's ear as I sat beside her.

She leaned into me, her warmth seeping through my sweater. "I know. I love you too." Then, with a mischievous grin, she turned to my father. "Now, about those 1930s photos…"

I groaned, but I was smiling. After all, we had all the time in the world for embarrassing photos and family stories. We were home.

*D*id you like this paranormal rom-com? If you'd like to read more paranormal rom-com from me, check out Her Gargoyle Protector, a paranormal rom-com set in the small town of Beastly Falls. Turn the page for a sneak peak!

HER GARGOYLE PROTECTOR
SNEAK PEAK

*A*mber

I drove down the winding forest road and glanced in my rearview mirror, wiping away tears for what felt like the millionth time today. My hands were shaking on the steering wheel, and my stomach growled loud enough to drown out the static-filled radio. The road was empty behind me, and I breathed a sigh of relief. Maybe I had finally ditched Kevin. When he had found me in that last town, I barely escaped before he caught me. I ducked out before the sun was even up to avoid him following me. But now I was running on fumes, needing caffeine and food and a new sanctuary.

I checked the map I had bought. Yes, it was a paper map. I didn't know they still made those. But it was a good thing because my GPS had started going haywire a few miles back. In fact, it showed nothing but green and a large body of water. Yet, it was clearly wrong because I was looking at a quaint sign that read "Welcome to Beastly Falls, Population???" in swirling golden script. Cute name.

The only problem was, it wasn't supposed to be here.

The GPS and the paper map agreed. There was no town supposed to be here, named Beastly Falls or not. This was an empty stretch of road for at least another hour. Yet there was a town. It may not be on my map, but at this point, I'd take any port in a storm. I hoped they had coffee strong enough to wake the dead, because that's exactly how I felt.

As I pulled into what looked like the main street, lined with the most adorable shops I had ever seen. It looked like a vintage New England town from postcards or the movies. I didn't think they existed. This was so far from my life in Baltimore, but I loved it already. I wondered if I could stay for a while. My eyes landed on a cozy little café called The Growling Bean. Charming. And hopefully not too on-the-nose about their coffee quality.

I parked my beat-up Corolla, grabbed my purse, and stepped out onto the sidewalk. That's when things got weird. Well, weirder.

Every single person on the street froze. And when I say froze, I mean like someone hit the pause button on a movie. But that wasn't even the strangest part. These weren't... people. At least, not entirely.

To my left stood a massive green creature that had more muscles than any body builder that I had ever seen and tusks coming out of his lower jaw. He wore a pinstriped, gray suit with a maroon tie and white dress shirt and was mid-bite into what looked like a gooey cinnamon bun. Beside him, there was a woman dressed in a green and brown homespun dress, with what looked like leaves and branches coming off of it, coming off of her, almost like she was part tree. It was very confusing. And they were staring at me. Because they weren't people. Weren't human. They were monsters.

I rubbed my eyes. Maybe I was more tired than I thought.

"Um, hi?" I managed weakly.

Silence. More staring.

Right. Okay. I remembered vaguely hearing about towns, usually outside of the big cities, that were populated with monsters, or supernaturals as they preferred to be called, since they were more comfortable living among their own kind. Monsters had been living among us for years, but we hadn't ever really known about them until a few decades ago. To say it had not gone well was an understatement, but most people handled it pretty well, though we only saw the occasional supernatural in the city, usually the more common ones, who looked like humans.

It was weird to be the one they would stare at, but I suppose it made sense, since I was probably the minority here, since I didn't see any humans on the street. This was fine. Totally normal. I could handle this. Besides, true monsters didn't always look that way on the outside. I knew that better than anyone. I'd just get my coffee and be on my way to wherever I was going next. Not that I had a clue where that would be.

I pushed open the café door, a little bell announcing my arrival. The low hum of conversation stopped dead inside and all eyes turned to me. The barista—who appeared to be part goat—dropped the mug he was holding, the ceramic shattering on the tile floor. I swallowed and made my way to the counter.

"Can I get a large coffee, please? Cream and sugar." I tried to sound normal, like I ordered from mythical creatures every day.

Before the goat-man could respond, the door burst open behind me. A short, plump woman with rosy cheeks and a head full of curls that defied gravity bustled in, pushing through the crowd of beings who had blocked the door, all staring at me. She maneuvered her way to my side and glared at everyone with exasperation.

"Oh, for heaven's sake, you lot! Have none of you ever seen a human before?" She turned to me with a warm smile, trying to appear grandmotherly. "I apologize, dear. We don't get many visitors here in Beastly Falls. I'm Sylvia Haasenfrau, the mayor."

I shook her offered hand, feeling like I'd stumbled into some bizarre dream. "Amber Lawson. Nice to meet you."

Sylvia shooed away the gawking crowd. "We're so happy to see you. You look so tired, dear. A coffee should fix you up in no time, along with something to eat. Wyn, has she ordered yet?"

I felt a bit like a pine tree buffeted by a windstorm. Sylvia was a force of nature, but the man behind the counter, Wyn, busied himself making my coffee, so I was grateful for the intervention. "Something to eat, dear?"

I scanned the menu on the board, almost too tired to read it. Since it was lunchtime, I settled for soup and half a sandwich, which I relayed. Wyn nodded, acknowledging my order, and handed over the mug of steaming coffee. It smelled like heaven. I dug for my money, but he shook his head. "On the house, miss."

"Thank you."

He smiled, a bit shyly. "Welcome to Beastly Falls."

Sylvia nodded approvingly and steered me towards a two-seat table by the window, glaring over my shoulder at the crowd, who dispersed with mumbles. We settled at the small wrought-iron table and I sipped my coffee. Oh, it was like tasting heaven. Or maybe I was exhausted. Either way, I was immensely grateful for the hit of caffeine flooding my veins.

Sylvia waited a few minutes, studying me, then she spoke. "So, how did you find our little town, Amber?"

"I drove here," I replied, gesturing out front to my car, confused by the question. Maybe I needed more caffeine, or she needed something. What a weird question.

"Hmm," Sylvia said, tapping her chin. "Forgive me for saying, but you look tuckered out, like you could use a good rest. Have you considered staying a while?"

I blinked. "I hadn't really thought about it. But this is a cute town."

Actually, I was tired of moving and had no actual destination in mind. This would be the last kind of town Kevin would ever come to, so it would be the perfect place to settle, at least for a while. And my bank account could use some funding, since I'd been draining it quickly, being on the run for the past few months. I wondered if they would have any job openings? I wasn't picky. It would be too much to ask for that they'd have a librarian position. I'd waitressed in college and worked retail too. I was no stranger to hard work.

Sylvia nodded sagely, folding her hands in front of her. "I can sense these things about people. Did you move recently?"

"You could say that," I mumbled, not wanting to get into the whole fleeing-my-abusive-ex story. It had always been my experience that most people didn't like when you got too personal right away. And when you add in an abusive ex, well, most people found themselves with a pressing appointment or something else to do really fast. No one wanted that kind of trouble. Not that I blamed them. I wish I could avoid this trouble too.

Sylvia, on the other hand, laid a comforting hand on my arm and relief flooded through me, easing my stress. I could feel my muscles relaxing in my shoulders and the tension bleeding out of me. I think my shoulders even lowered from the vicinity of my ears, something they hadn't done in weeks. I could breathe for the first time in so long without the band around my chest. There was something about her that made me wonder who or what she was. While she looked human, I didn't think she was.

Her eyes were kind as she looked at me and I got the sense she knew what was going on. "You don't need to keep running, dear. You're safe here for as long as you stay with us. You seem like you could use a break. We have a lovely bed-and-breakfast owned by Esme Red, just down the street, with a room for rent that might suit you just fine."

I was feeling a bit bewildered, but maybe that was the stress, lack of sleep, and hunger talking. Maybe I had driven into an alternate reality, but I was feeling better, almost like I truly was safe, like Kevin couldn't get to me here and I could take a chance at staying for a while. I needed to replenish my savings, anyway. "That would be great."

Wyn brought my soup and sandwich, along with a salad for Sylvia, and we ate quietly. All the while, I felt like a sideshow attraction with large numbers of onlookers coming into the cafe or walking by and staring at me, deliberately ignoring Mayor Sylvia's pointed glare or even more obvious comments for them to move along. As strange as it all was, it also comforted me. If they reacted to me, a stranger, like this, Kevin could never sneak into Beastly Falls. I would have some warning and be able to escape if he did.

Once I finished eating, I scanned the street, looking at the quaint facades of the shops all along the street. They were all a bit distorted, as if seen through a mirror, by defying the laws of nature. But the brick and stone structures, and canopies were so lovely, I couldn't wait to explore, and hopefully find a job.

I felt a tug towards a stone building in the distance, a beautiful gothic structure a couple of streets away. It was a couple of stories taller than some of the other buildings, standing separately from all other structures, and it had a lone figure standing on the roof.

"What is that building?"

Sylvia followed my gaze. "That's our library. It's open twenty-four hours because we have a lot of nocturnal residents, though we haven't had a nighttime librarian for a while, so there are times when it's closed at night. Do you like to read?"

A library? A town that needs a librarian? It was almost too good to be true. "Something like that," I replied. "Would you be able to direct me to the bed-and-breakfast? I'd love to see if I could get a room."

Sylvia beamed. "Of course. You must be exhausted. I'll take you there now."

We cleared our table, and she ushered me out of the café, chattering about the town's history. As we walked and she pointed out landmarks, I wondered just what I'd gotten myself into. But for the first time in months, I had a glimmer of hope. Maybe, just maybe, Beastly Falls was exactly where I needed to be.

❄

If you'd like to read more, click Her Gargoyle Protector.

ALSO BY SABRINA SILVERS

THE DIRIGO PACK SERIES

The Dirigo Pack. One of the prominent wolf shifter packs in the United States. Led by Duncan MacKinnon and his family of three sons and a daughter, they're dedicated to protecting their family, their pack, and living a life of honor. But they face their greatest adversary when Kayleigh MacKinnon is kidnapped by an unknown enemy and they face treachery among other packs. Only through love and the strongest of will can they survive.

Forbidden Moon (Prequel) Can a mating bond bridge the gap between feuding packs ... or will it destroy them all?

Maya Wessex and Garrett Colvin were childhood friends until their pack rivalry tore then apart. When they meet again as adults, the mating bond roars to life, giving them a second chance at life, love, and mating.

Alpha's Moon (Book 1) The Alpha-Heir and a hybrid shifter-witch unite to find the Pack Princess when she's kidnapped by an old enemy. They must fight their mating urges and challenges from within the pack and the enemies outside to find their love and save his sister.

Moon Madness (Book 2) A wolf who almost lost control of his beast must dive into the belly of shifter politics with a tough female enforcer as a body guard to protect his pack and save his sister. While navigating politics, they must overcome their own prejudices and attraction, while fighting the knives aimed at their back to save their pack.

Feral Moon (Book 3) An Alpha slowly losing his mind to moon madness and a lack of mate is given a mate through treachery and deceit, only to find the kidnapped princess of his rival is the mate who can save him. Will he keep her and risk war or will he let her go and lose himself to the madness that will destroy him and his pack, and possibly all of the shifter world?

Rejected Moon (Book 4) As Nik and Isa confront the mating bond that ties them together, can they navigate the dangers of their present, and overcome the pain of their past to find a new future, healed and whole together? Or will they fall back into despair, alone and broken? Rejected.

Orc World Series

Rescued By Her Monster Mercenaries (Villains Do It Better series)

Trapped in a realm straight out of a fantasy novel? Check. Sold off as a mate in a bizarre auction? Double check. And guess what? The bidders aren't charming princes but rather orcs, minotaurs, and other creatures straight out of my worst nightmares.

As if my love life wasn't complicated enough, we've got malevolent forces lurking around, threatening to ruin our newfound romance. But hey, at least I've got two strapping warriors by my side. Who needs a knight in shining armor when you've got an orc and a minotaur?

Now, the big question looms: Do I try to find my way back home or do I stay in this fantastical world with my unlikely mates? Love, danger, and some seriously weird creatures await.

Collected by the Orc (Orcs Unbound)

After my boss makes a pass at me during an outdoor leadership retreat, I somehow get lost in the Colorado woods and end up in a weird fantasy world right out of Lord of the Rings, complete with orcs! Only this orc is sexy and protective, saying he'll help me get home.

As we journey through his world and he shows a softer side, not to mention a smokin' hot sexy side, I begin to wonder if it would be that bad to stay here.

But I sense he's keeping secrets and, when a dethroned orc prince and his band of merry rebels show up to kill my escort for crimes against the people, should I defend my protector or run screaming into the night?

ABOUT SABRINA SILVERS

Sabrina Silvers began her writing career dreaming of elves, orcs, and hobbits in the fantasy section of her local library, looking in wardrobes for Narnia and Aslan, and hunting for gnomes in the forest. To her dismay, she never found any of them except between the pages of her books. So, she had to go out and create them for herself, leading to her lifelong love of reading and writing and dreaming about adventures, fantasy creatures and love in fantasy lands! She divides her time between writing sexy contemporary romances under a different pen name, reading, knitting and being owned by a very spoiled cocker spaniel who does not share her love of fantasy creatures.

For upcoming releases and other information including access to bonus content, sign up for her newsletter at her website at: https://www.sabrinasilvers.com

- facebook.com/SabrinaSilversAuthor
- instagram.com/sabrinasilversauthor
- tiktok.com/@sabrinasilversauthor
- amazon.com/stores/Sabrina-Silvers/author/B08XGWXHF8
- bookbub.com/authors/sabrina-silvers
- goodreads.com/sabrina_silversauthor

Printed in Great Britain
by Amazon